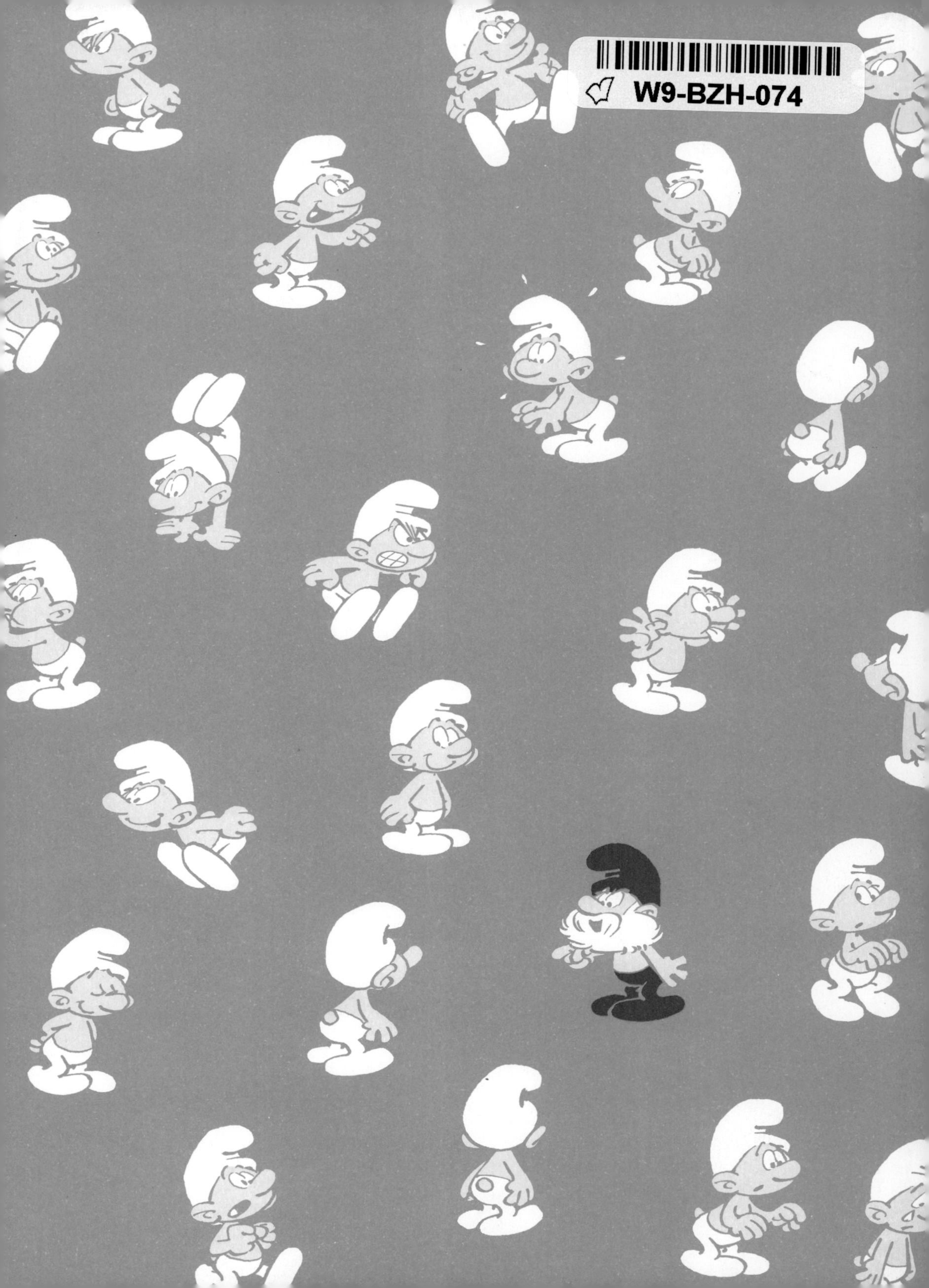

THE
STRANGE AWAKENING
OF LAZY SMURF

Peyo

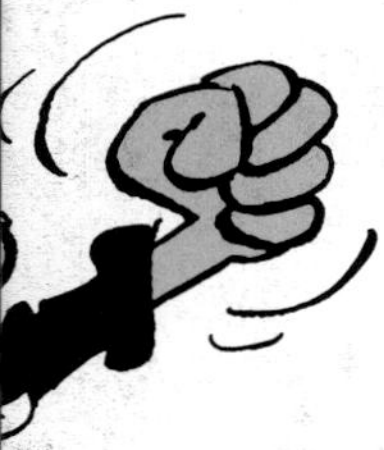

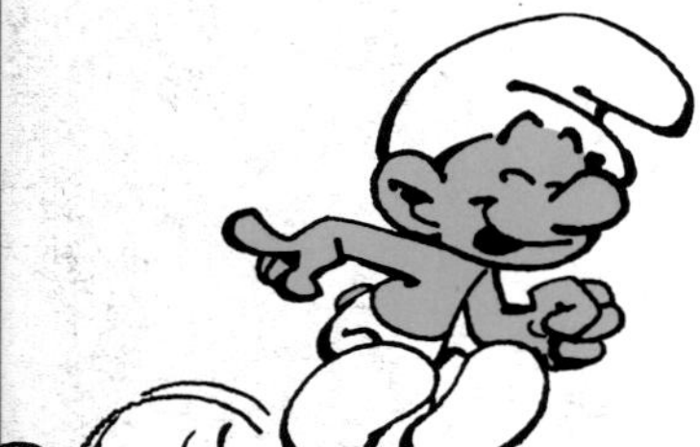

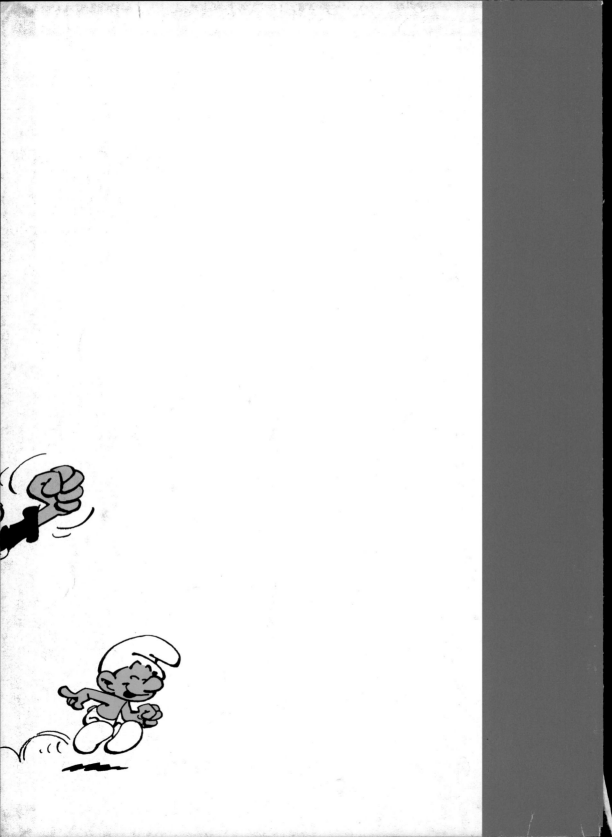

THE STRANGE AWAKENING OF LAZY SMURF

What are you smurfing?
We're smurfing a joke on Lazy Smurf, Papa Smurf. We want to make him think he's been asleep for two hundred years!
Heh heh! How far will they smurf with all this?
Hey! Here are the fake beards!
Hurry up! He's going to smurf up soon!
WHAAAA!
I slept good!... But what's with all these mushrooms?!
And my curtains? Yuck! They're full of spider smurfs! What's happened?
!
2

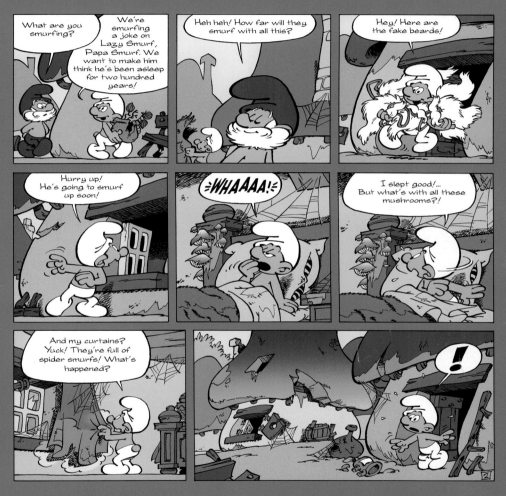

A SMURFS GRAPHIC NOVEL BY PEYO

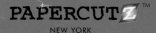

PAPERCUTZ™
NEW YORK

SMURFS GRAPHIC NOVELS AVAILABLE FROM PAPERCUTZ™

1. THE PURPLE SMURFS
2. THE SMURFS AND THE MAGIC FLUTE
3. THE SMURF KING
4. THE SMURFETTE
5. THE SMURFS AND THE EGG
6. THE SMURFS AND THE HOWLIBIRD
7. THE ASTROSMURF
8. THE SMURF APPRENTICE
9. GARGAMEL AND THE SMURFS
10. THE RETURN OF THE SMURFETTE
11. THE SMURF OLYMPICS
12. SMURF VS. SMURF
13. SMURF SOUP
14. THE BABY SMURF
15. THE SMURFLINGS
16. THE AEROSMURF
17. THE STRANGE AWAKENING
    OF LAZY SMURF
- THE SMURF CHRISTMAS

COMING SOON:

18. THE FINANCE SMURF
- FOREVER SMURFETTE

THE SMURFS graphic novels are available in paperback for $5.99 each and in hardcover for $10.99 each at booksellers everywhere. You can also order online at papercutz.com. Or call 1-800-886-1223, Monday through Friday, 9 – 5 EST. MC, Visa, and AmEx accepted. To order by mail, please add $4.00 for postage and handling for first book ordered, $1.00 for each additional book and make check payable to NBM Publishing. Send to: Papercutz, 160 Broadway, Suite 700, East Wing, New York, NY 10038.

THE SMURFS graphic novels are also available digitally wherever e-books are sold.

PAPERCUTZ.COM

THE STRANGE AWAKENING OF LAZY SMURF

SCHLUMPF I PUFFI PITUFO SCHTROUMPF © Peyo - 2014 - Licensed through Lafig Belgium - www.smurf.com

English translation copyright © 2014 by Papercutz.
All rights reserved.

"The Strange Awakening of Lazy Smurf"
BY PEYO

"Gargamel and his Nephews"
BY PEYO

"Gargamel's Twin"
BY PEYO

"The Ogre and the Smurfs"
BY PEYO

"Disco Smurf"
BY PEYO

"Surfing Smurf"
BY PEYO

Joe Johnson, SMURFLATIONS
Adam Grano, SMURFIC DESIGN
Janice Chiang, LETTERING SMURFETTE
Matt. Murray, SMURF CONSULTANT
Beth Scorzato, SMURF COORDINATOR
Bryce Gold, SMURF INTERN
Michael Petranek, ASSOCIATE SMURF
Jim Salicrup, SMURF-IN-CHIEF

PAPERBACK EDITION ISBN: 978-1-59707-509-1
HARDCOVER EDITION ISBN: 978-1-59707-510-7

PRINTED IN CHINA MARCH 2014 BY WKT CO. LTD.
3/F PHASE I LEADER INDUSTRIAL CENTRE
188 TEXACO ROAD, TSEUN WAN, N.T., HONG KONG

Papercutz books may be purchased for business or promotional use. For information on bulk purchases please contact Macmillan Corporate and Premium Sales Department at (800) 221-7945 x5442.

DISTRIBUTED BY MACMILLAN
FIRST PAPERCUTZ PRINTING

J Peyo

THE STRANGE AWAKENING OF LAZY SMURF

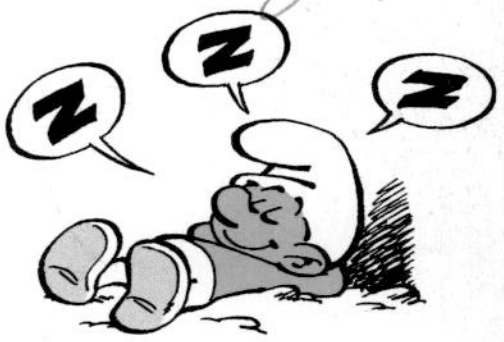
Z
Z
Z

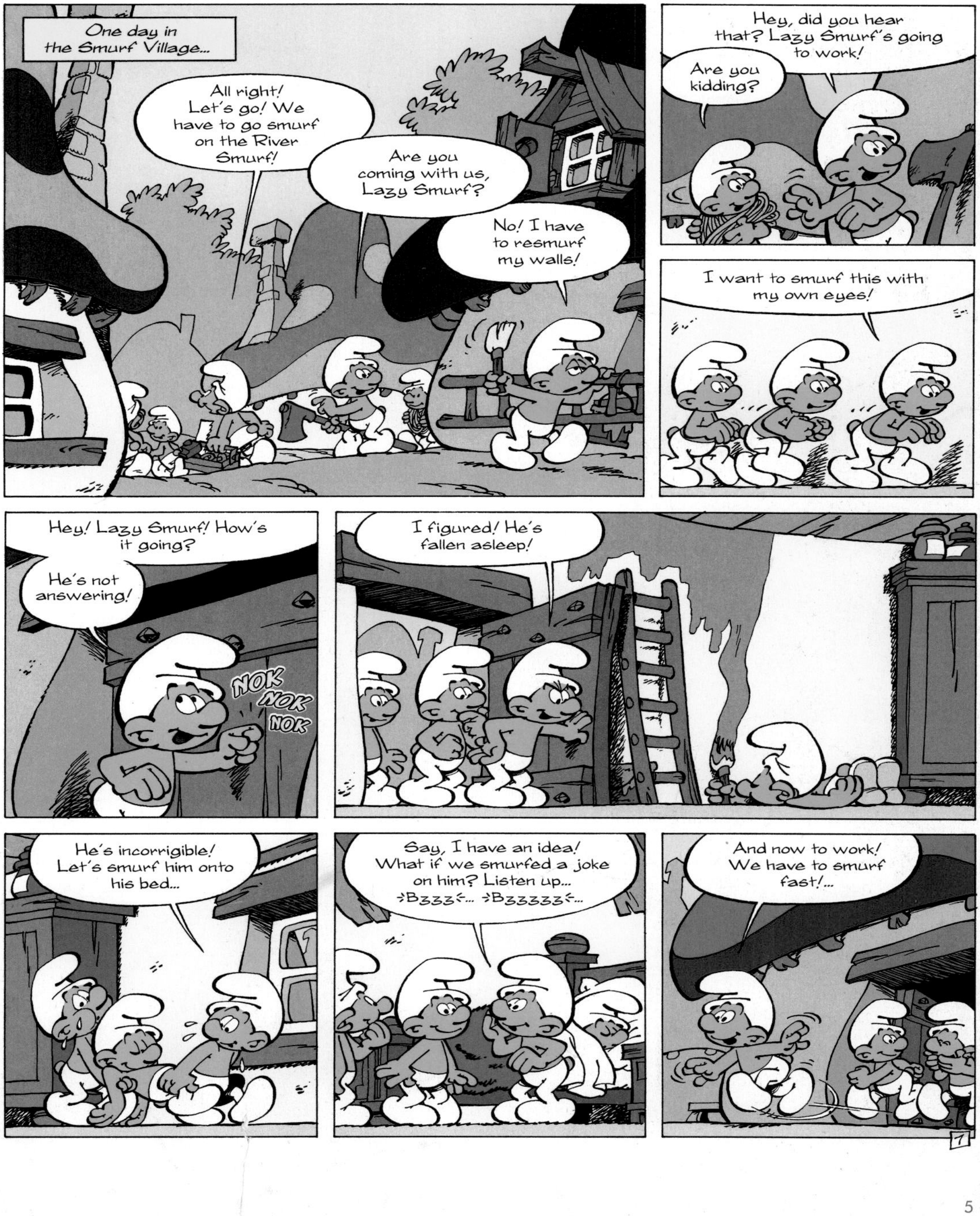
One day in the Smurf Village...
All right! Let's go! We have to go smurf on the River Smurf!
Are you coming with us, Lazy Smurf?
No! I have to resmurf my walls!
Hey, did you hear that? Lazy Smurf's going to work!
Are you kidding?
I want to smurf this with my own eyes!
Hey! Lazy Smurf! How's it going?
He's not answering!
NOK NOK NOK
I figured! He's fallen asleep!
He's incorrigible! Let's smurf him onto his bed...
Say, I have an idea! What if we smurfed a joke on him? Listen up...
Bzzz... Bzzzzz...
And now to work! We have to smurf fast!...
1

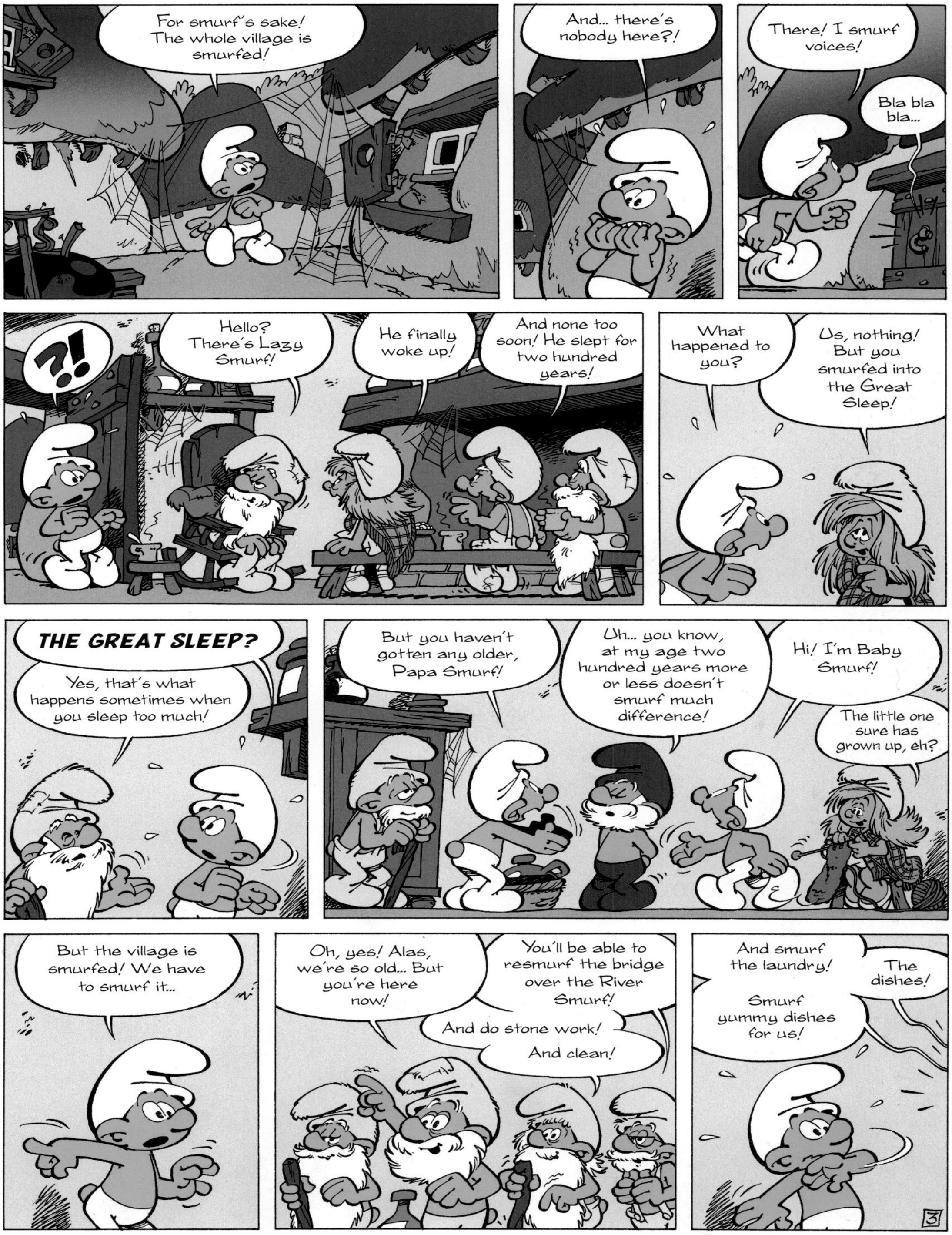

For smurf's sake! The whole village is smurfed!
And... there's nobody here?!
There! I smurf voices!
Bla bla bla...
?!
Hello? There's Lazy Smurf!
He finally woke up!
And none too soon! He slept for two hundred years!
What happened to you?
Us, nothing! But you smurfed into the Great Sleep!
THE GREAT SLEEP?
Yes, that's what happens sometimes when you sleep too much!
But you haven't gotten any older, Papa Smurf!
Uh... you know, at my age two hundred years more or less doesn't smurf much difference!
Hi! I'm Baby Smurf!
The little one sure has grown up, eh?
But the village is smurfed! We have to smurf it...
Oh, yes! Alas, we're so old... But you're here now!
You'll be able to resmurf the bridge over the River Smurf!
And do stone work!
And clean!
And smurf the laundry!
The dishes!
Smurf yummy dishes for us!
3

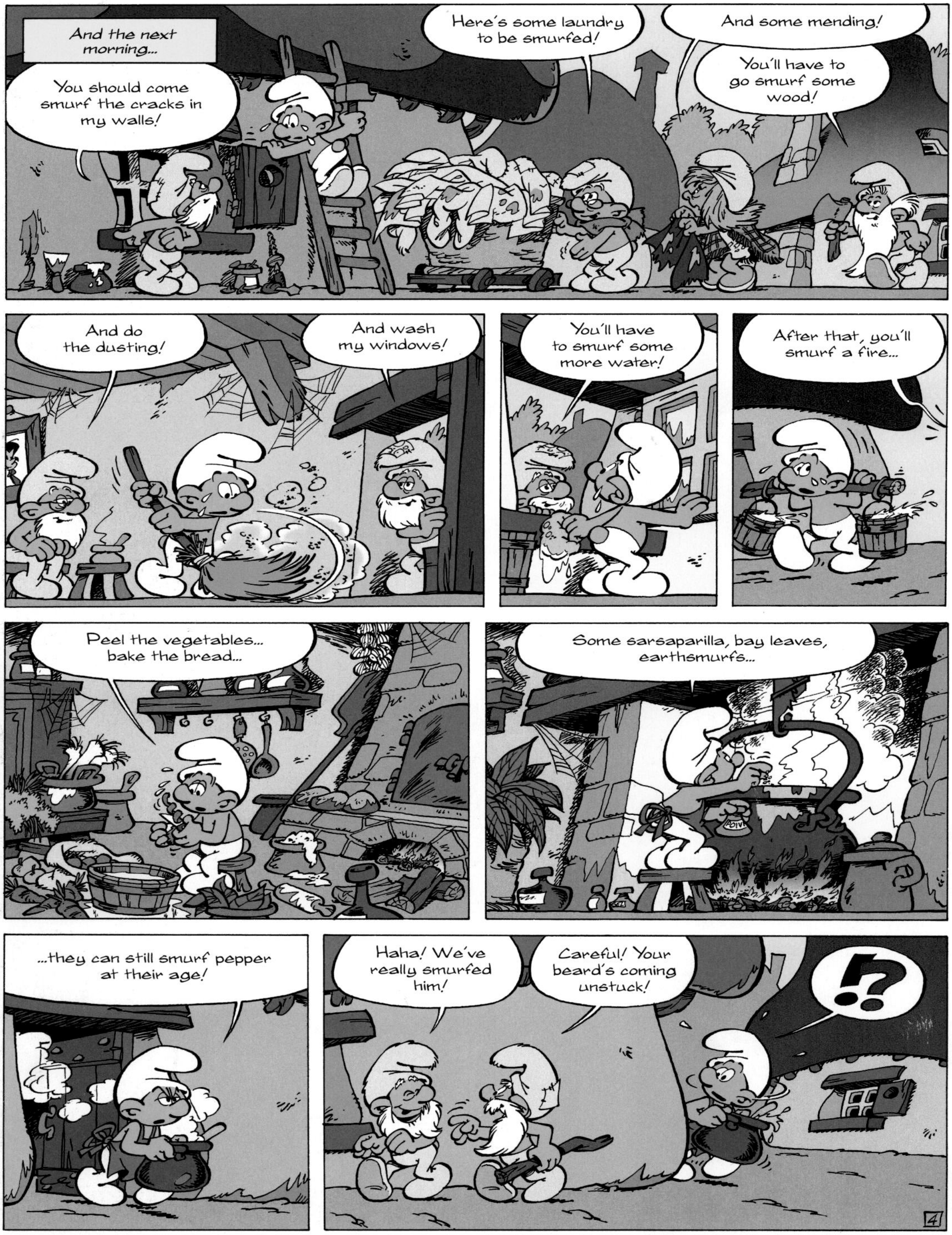
And the next morning...
You should come smurf the cracks in my walls!
Here's some laundry to be smurfed!
And some mending!
You'll have to go smurf some wood!
And do the dusting!
And wash my windows!
You'll have to smurf some more water!
After that, you'll smurf a fire...
Peel the vegetables... bake the bread...
Some sarsaparilla, bay leaves, earthsmurfs...
...they can still smurf pepper at their age!
Haha! We've really smurfed him!
Careful! Your beard's coming unstuck!
!?
4

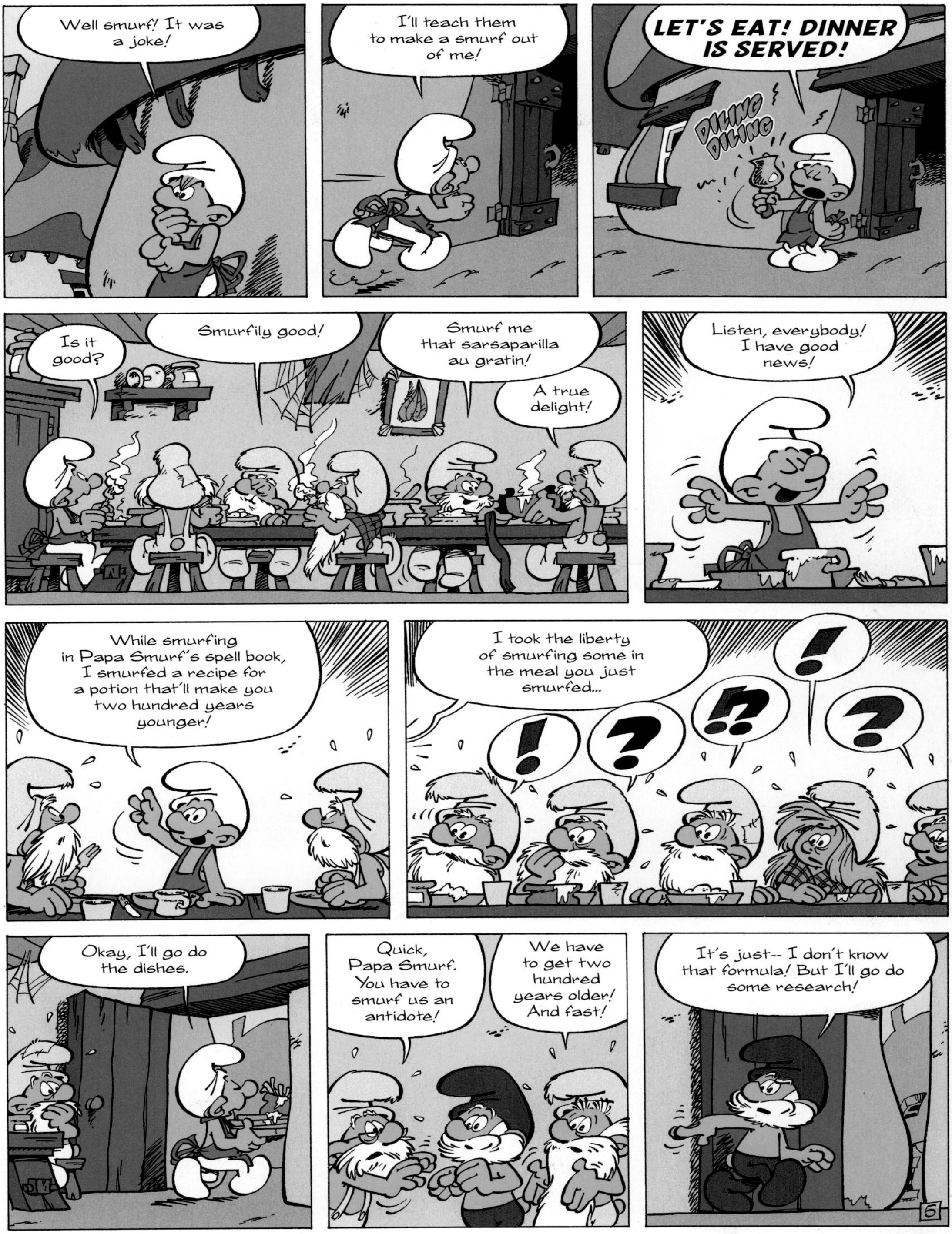

Well smurf! It was a joke!
I'll teach them to make a smurf out of me!
LET'S EAT! DINNER IS SERVED!
DILING DILING
Is it good?
Smurfily good!
Smurf me that sarsaparilla au gratin!
A true delight!
Listen, everybody! I have good news!
While smurfing in Papa Smurf's spell book, I smurfed a recipe for a potion that'll make you two hundred years younger!
I took the liberty of smurfing some in the meal you just smurfed...
!
?
!?
?
Okay, I'll go do the dishes.
Quick, Papa Smurf. You have to smurf us an antidote!
We have to get two hundred years older! And fast!
It's just-- I don't know that formula! But I'll go do some research!
5

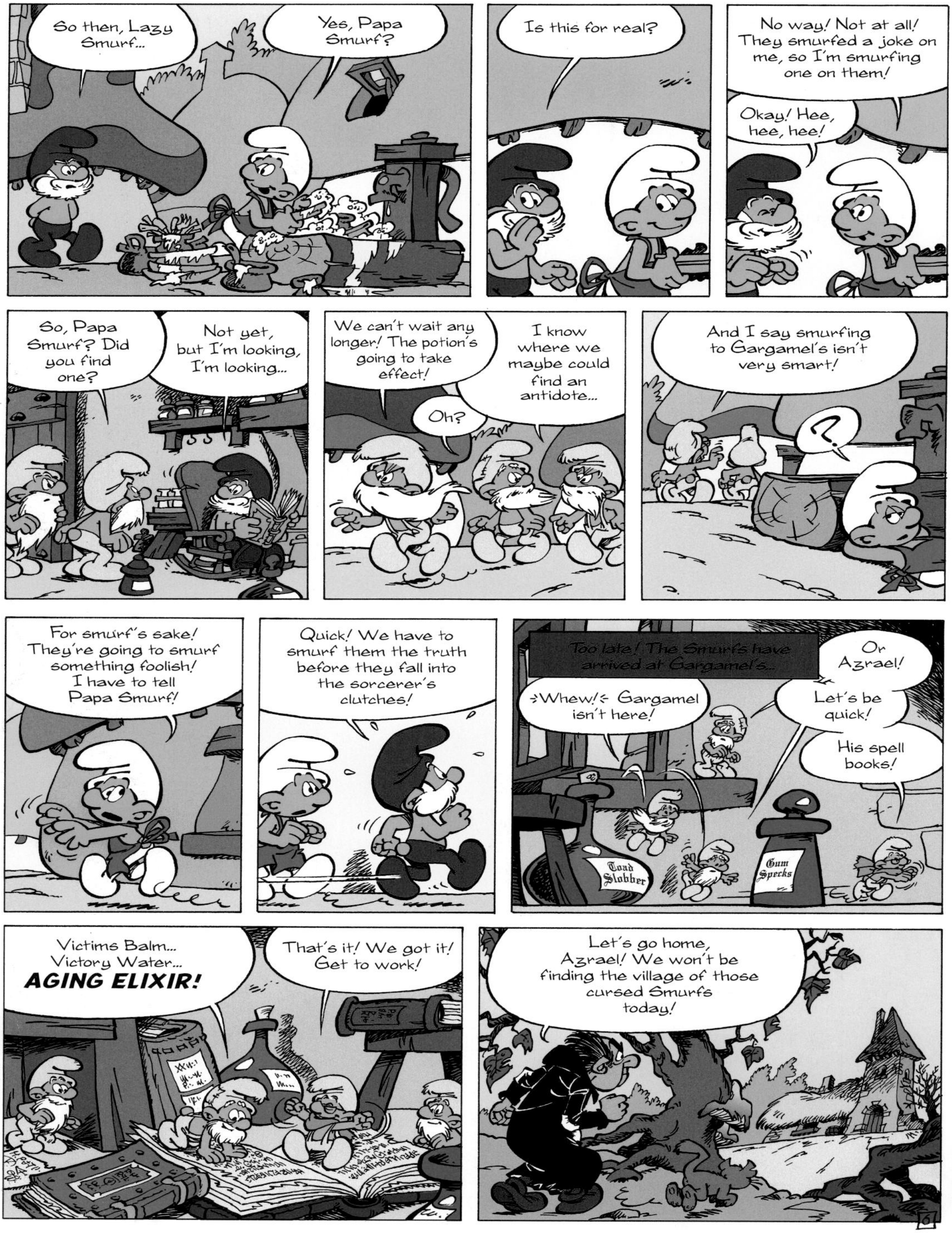
So then, Lazy Smurf...
Yes, Papa Smurf?
Is this for real?
No way! Not at all! They smurfed a joke on me, so I'm smurfing one on them!
Okay! Hee, hee, hee!
So, Papa Smurf? Did you find one?
Not yet, but I'm looking, I'm looking...
We can't wait any longer! The potion's going to take effect!
I know where we maybe could find an antidote...
Oh?
And I say smurfing to Gargamel's isn't very smart!
?
For smurf's sake! They're going to smurf something foolish! I have to tell Papa Smurf!
Quick! We have to smurf them the truth before they fall into the sorcerer's clutches!
Too late! The Smurfs have arrived at Gargamel's...
Whew! Gargamel isn't here!
Or Azrael!
Let's be quick!
His spell books!
Toad Slobber
Victims Balm... Victory Water... AGING ELIXIR!
That's it! We got it! Get to work!
Let's go home, Azrael! We won't be finding the village of those cursed Smurfs today!

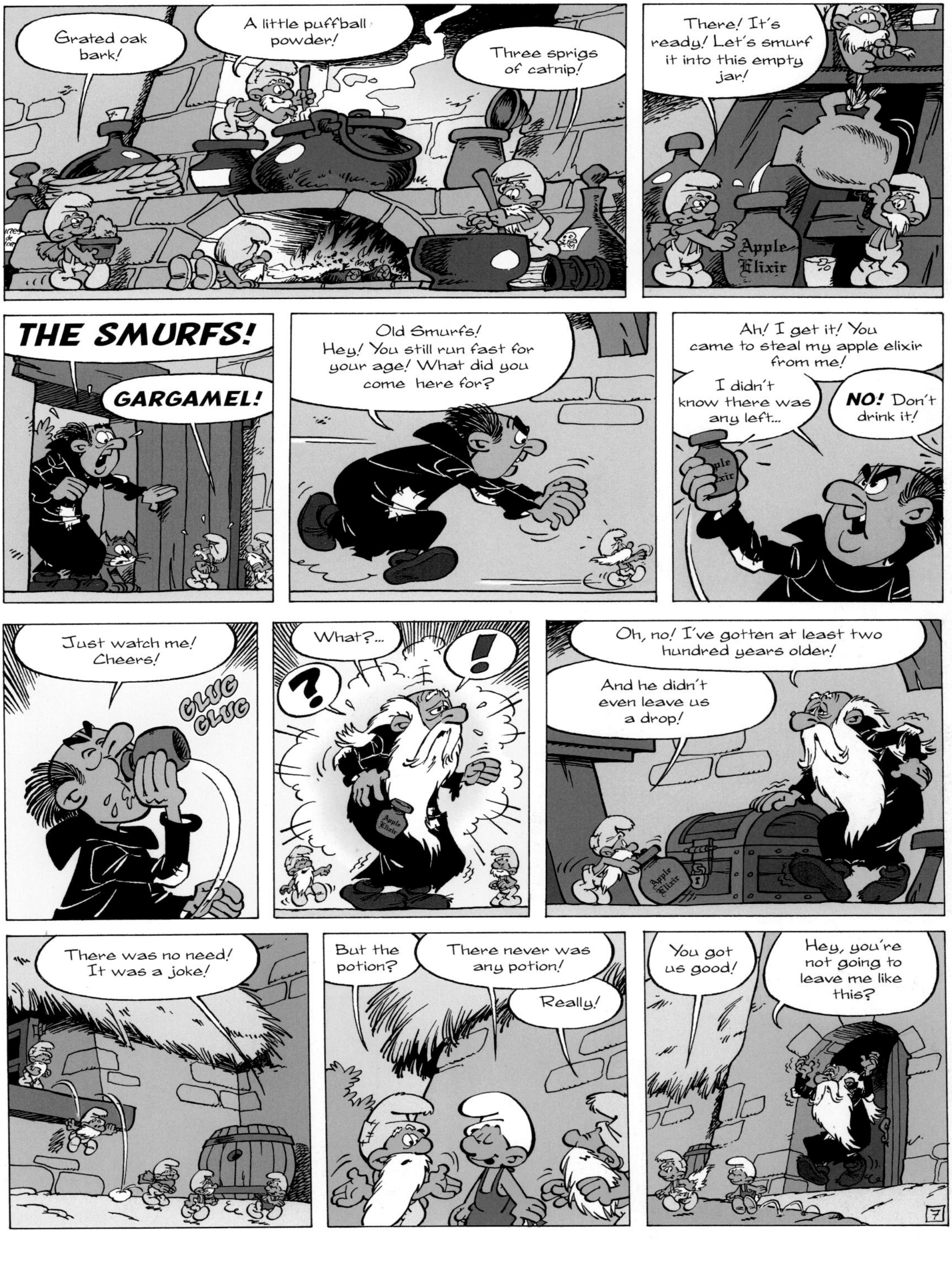

Grated oak bark!
A little puffball powder!
Three sprigs of catnip!
There! It's ready! Let's smurf it into this empty jar!
Apple Elixir
THE SMURFS!
GARGAMEL!
Old Smurfs! Hey! You still run fast for your age! What did you come here for?
Ah! I get it! You came to steal my apple elixir from me!
I didn't know there was any left...
NO! Don't drink it!
Just watch me! Cheers!
GLUG GLUG
What?...
?
!
Oh, no! I've gotten at least two hundred years older!
And he didn't even leave us a drop!
Apple Elixir
There was no need! It was a joke!
But the potion?
There never was any potion!
Really!
You got us good!
Hey, you're not going to leave me like this?
7

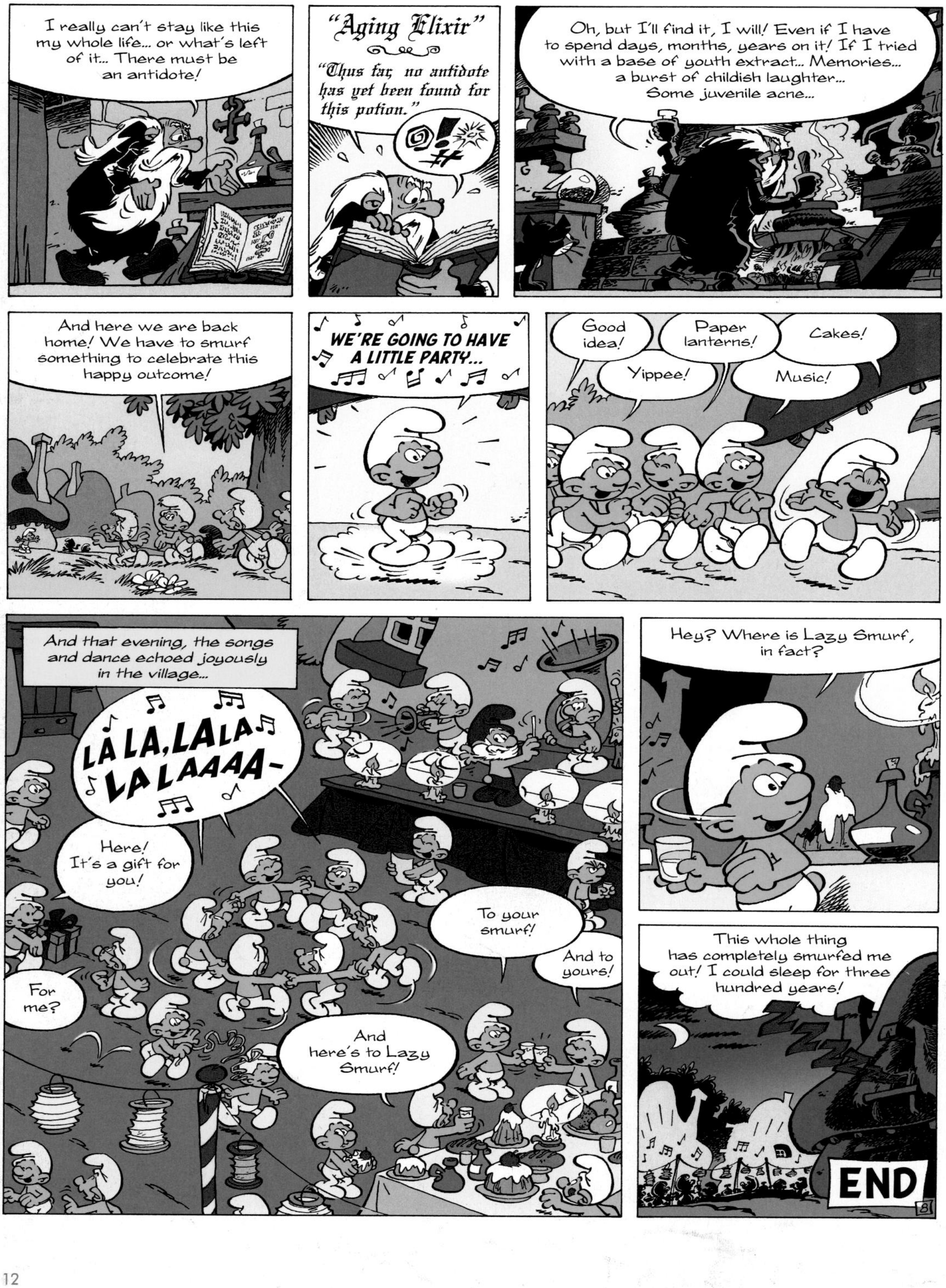
I really can't stay like this my whole life... or what's left of it... There must be an antidote!
"Aging Elixir"
"Thus far, no antidote has yet been found for this potion."
Oh, but I'll find it, I will! Even if I have to spend days, months, years on it! If I tried with a base of youth extract... Memories... a burst of childish laughter... Some juvenile acne...
And here we are back home! We have to smurf something to celebrate this happy outcome!
WE'RE GOING TO HAVE A LITTLE PARTY...
Good idea!
Paper lanterns!
Cakes!
Yippee!
Music!
And that evening, the songs and dance echoed joyously in the village...
LA LA, LALA LA LAAAA-
Here! It's a gift for you!
For me?
To your smurf!
And to yours!
And here's to Lazy Smurf!
Hey? Where is Lazy Smurf, in fact?
This whole thing has completely smurfed me out! I could sleep for three hundred years!
END

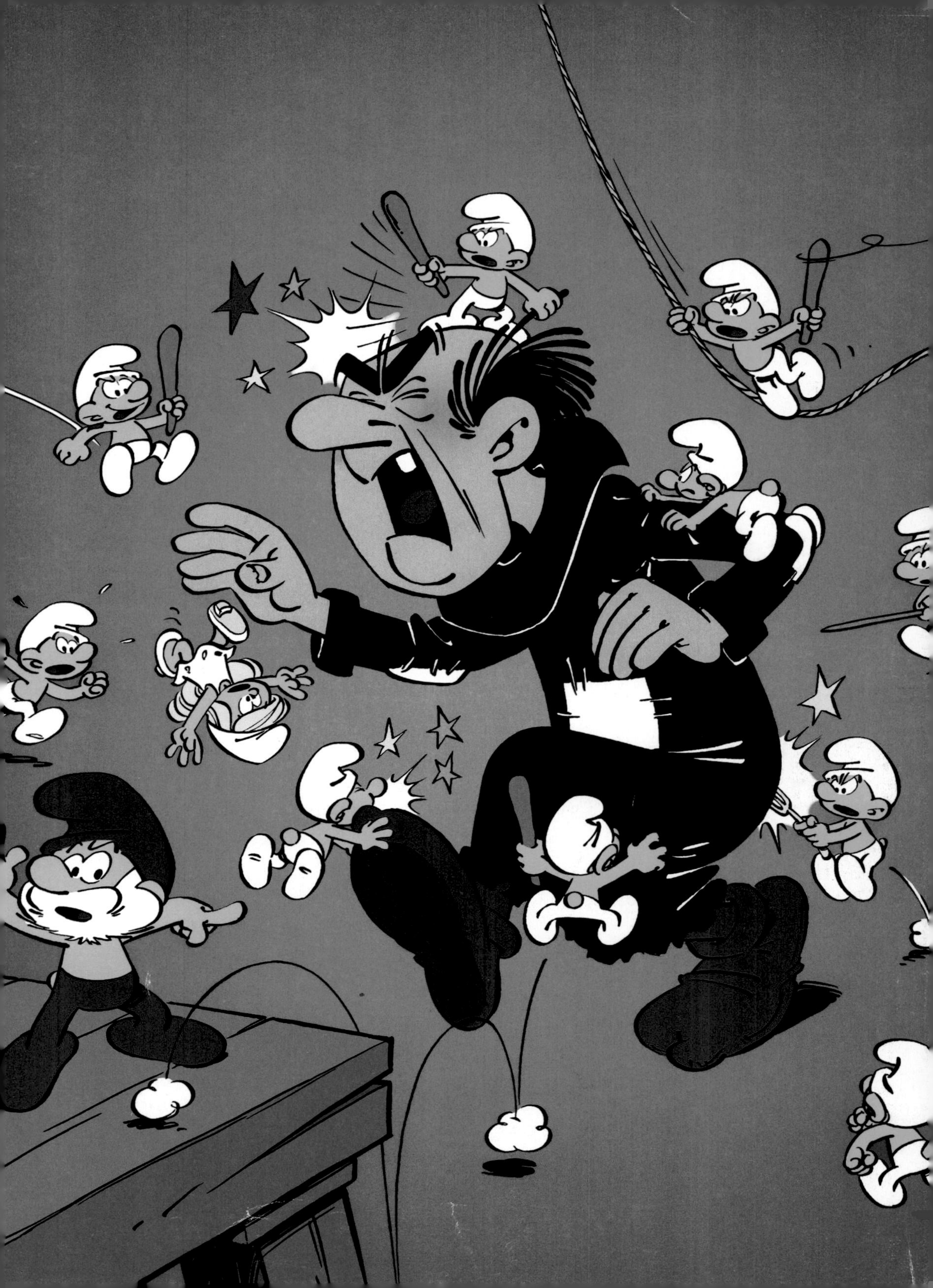

DISCO SMURF

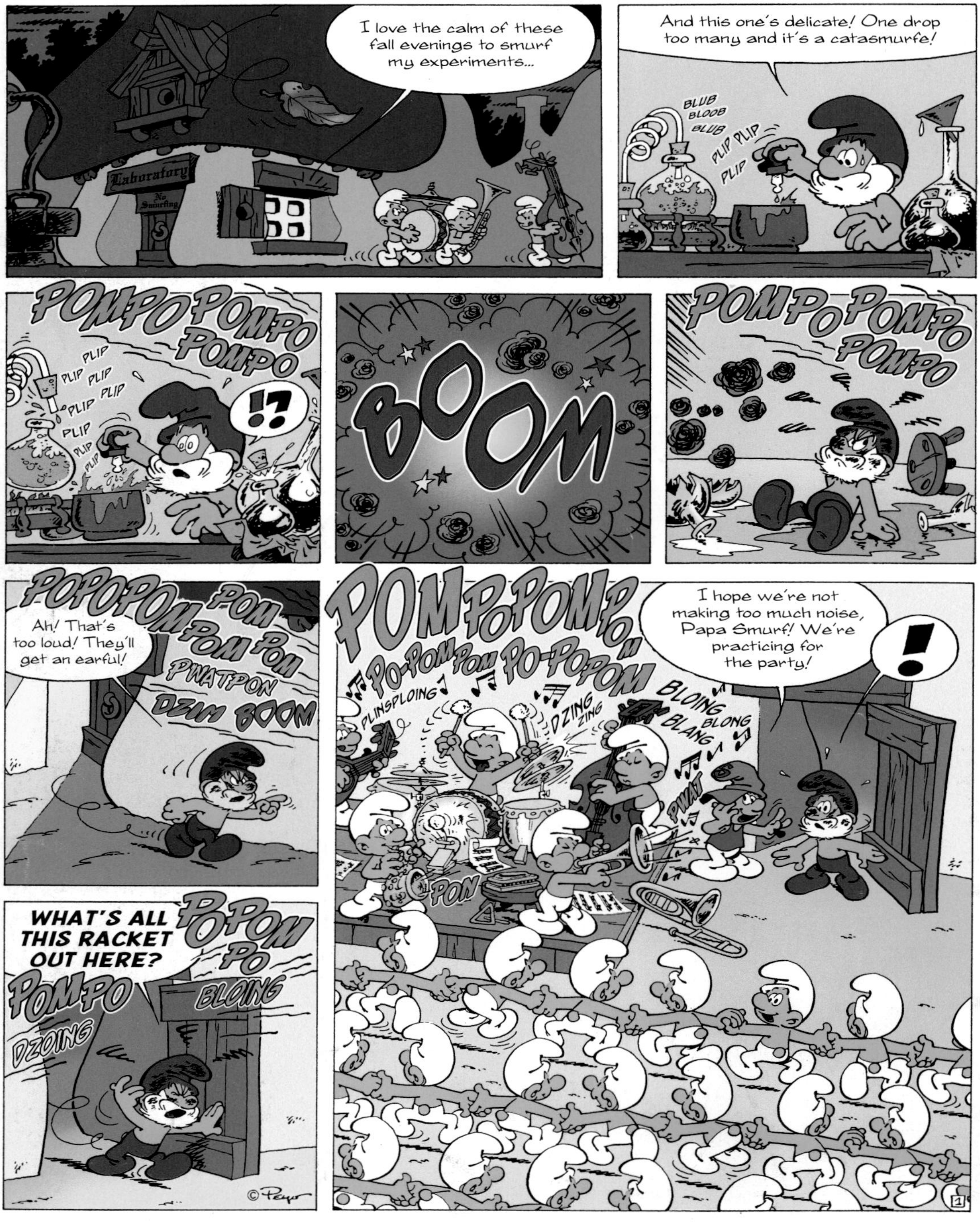

Laboratory
No Smurfing
I love the calm of these fall evenings to smurf my experiments...
And this one's delicate! One drop too many and it's a catasmurfe!
BLUB BLOOB BLUB
PLIP PLIP PLIP
POMPOPOMPO POMPO
PLIP PLIP PLIP PLIP PLIP PLIP PLIP
!?
BOOM
POMPOPOMPO POMPO
POPOPOM POM POMPOM POM
P'WATPON
DZIM BOOM
Ah! That's too loud! They'll get an earful!
WHAT'S ALL THIS RACKET OUT HERE?
POPOM PO
POMPO
BLOING
DZOING
POMPOPOMPOM
PO-POM POM PO-POPOM
PLINSPLOING
DZING ZING
BLOING BLONG BLANG
I hope we're not making too much noise, Papa Smurf! We're practicing for the party!
!
PWAT
PON

© Peyo

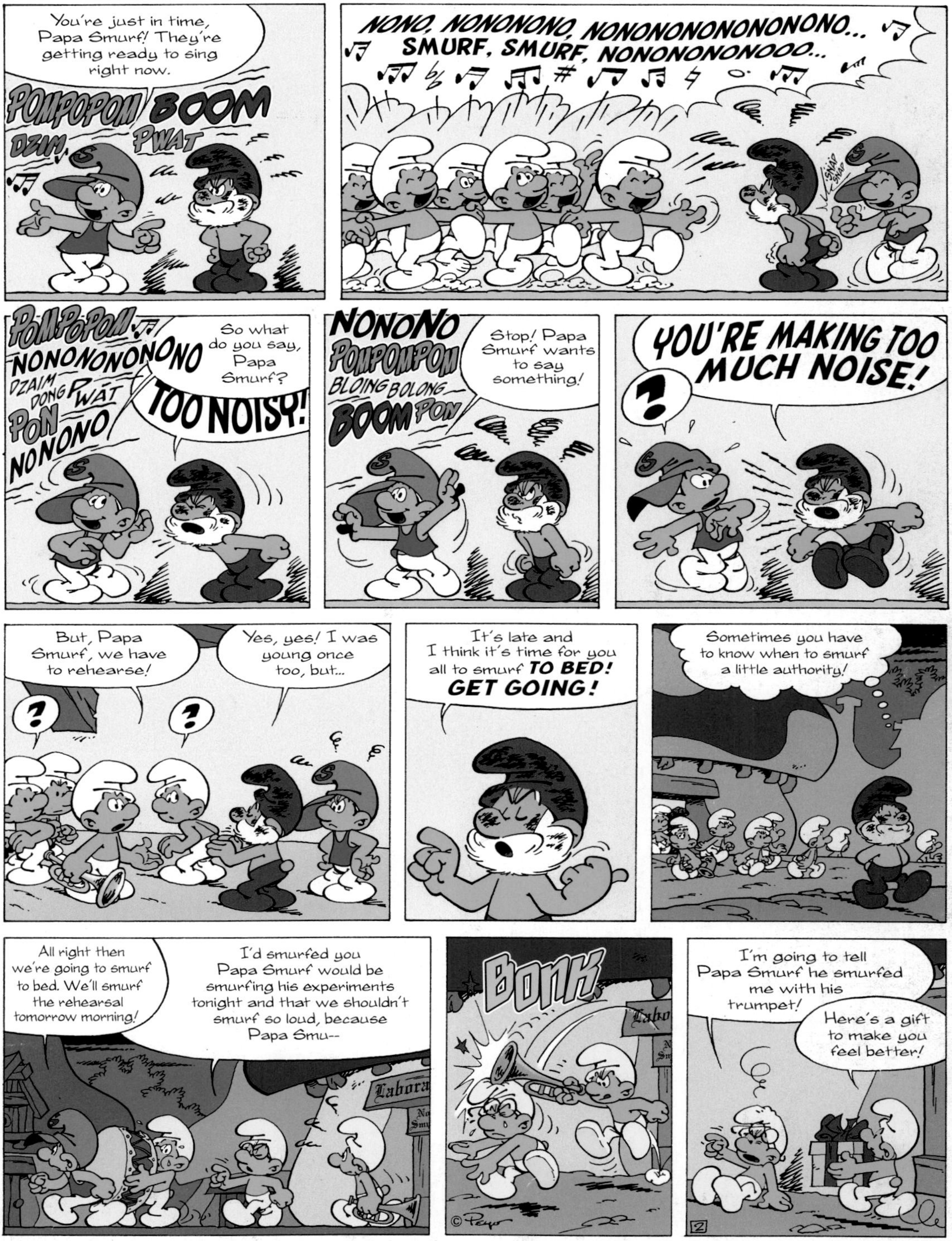
You're just in time, Papa Smurf! They're getting ready to sing right now.
POMPOPOM BOOM
DZIM PWAT
NONO, NONONONO, NONONONONONONONO...
SMURF, SMURF, NONONONONOOO...
SNAP SNAP
POMPOPOM
NONONONONONONO
DZAIM DONG PWAT
PON NONONO
So what do you say, Papa Smurf?
TOO NOISY!
NONONO
POMPOMPOM
BLOING BOLONG
BOOM PON
Stop! Papa Smurf wants to say something!
YOU'RE MAKING TOO MUCH NOISE!
But, Papa Smurf, we have to rehearse!
Yes, yes! I was young once too, but...
It's late and I think it's time for you all to smurf TO BED! GET GOING!
Sometimes you have to know when to smurf a little authority!
All right then we're going to smurf to bed. We'll smurf the rehearsal tomorrow morning!
I'd smurfed you Papa Smurf would be smurfing his experiments tonight and that we shouldn't smurf so loud, because Papa Smu--
BONK
I'm going to tell Papa Smurf he smurfed me with his trumpet!
Here's a gift to make you feel better!
© Peyo

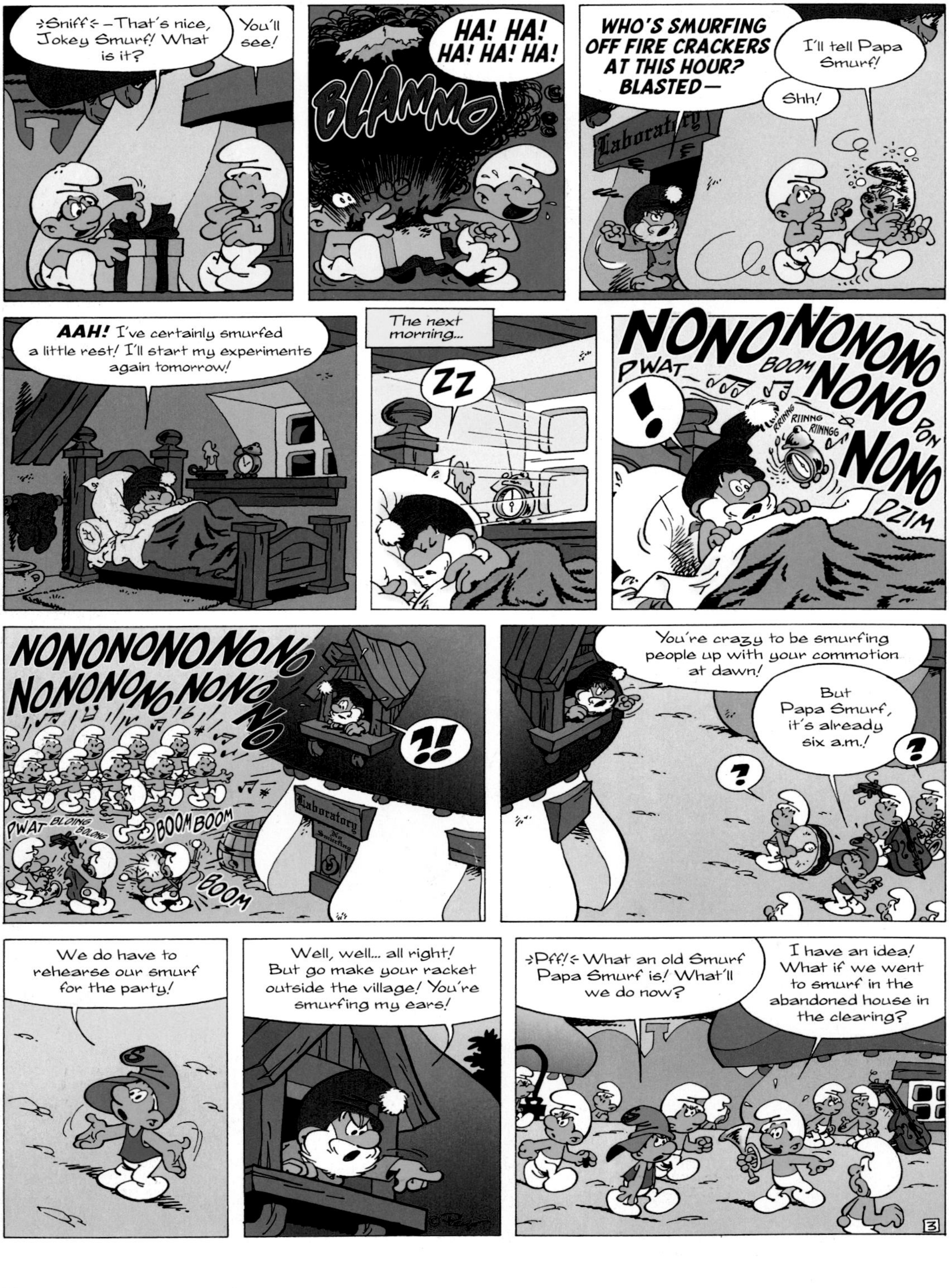

-Sniff- -That's nice, Jokey Smurf! What is it?
You'll see!
HA! HA! HA! HA! HA!
BLAMMO
WHO'S SMURFING OFF FIRE CRACKERS AT THIS HOUR? BLASTED—
I'll tell Papa Smurf!
Shh!
Laboratory
AAH! I've certainly smurfed a little rest! I'll start my experiments again tomorrow!
The next morning...
ZZ
NONONONONONO
PWAT
BOOM
NONO
RIINNG
RIINNG
RIINNGG
PON
NONO
!
DZIM
NONONONONONONO
NONONONONONONO
?!
Laboratory
No Smurfing
PWAT
BLOING
BOLONG
BOOM BOOM
BOOM
You're crazy to be smurfing people up with your commotion at dawn!
But Papa Smurf, it's already six a.m.!
?
?
We do have to rehearse our smurf for the party!
Well, well... all right! But go make your racket outside the village! You're smurfing my ears!
-Pff!- What an old Smurf Papa Smurf is! What'll we do now?
I have an idea! What if we went to smurf in the abandoned house in the clearing?
3

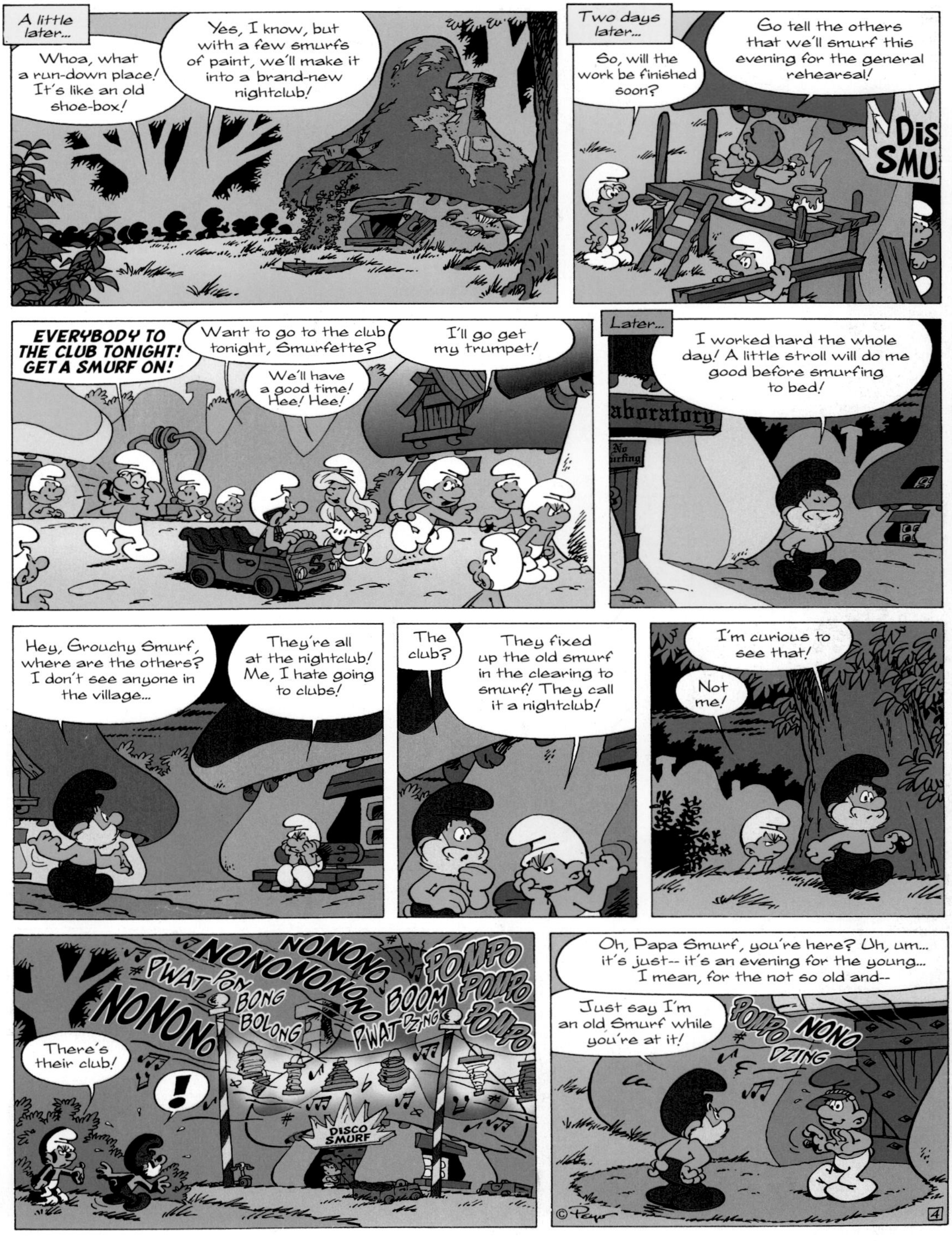
A little later...
Whoa, what a run-down place! It's like an old shoe-box!
Yes, I know, but with a few smurfs of paint, we'll make it into a brand-new nightclub!
Two days later...
So, will the work be finished soon?
Go tell the others that we'll smurf this evening for the general rehearsal!
DIS SMU
EVERYBODY TO THE CLUB TONIGHT! GET A SMURF ON!
Want to go to the club tonight, Smurfette?
We'll have a good time! Hee! Hee!
I'll go get my trumpet!
Later...
I worked hard the whole day! A little stroll will do me good before smurfing to bed!
Laboratory
No Smurfing
Hey, Grouchy Smurf, where are the others? I don't see anyone in the village...
They're all at the nightclub! Me, I hate going to clubs!
The club?
They fixed up the old smurf in the clearing to smurf! They call it a nightclub!
I'm curious to see that!
Not me!
NONONO NONONONONONO PWAT PON BONG BOLONG NONONO BOOM PWAT DZING POMPO POMPO POMPO
There's their club!
!
DISCO SMURF
Oh, Papa Smurf, you're here? Uh, um... it's just-- it's an evening for the young... I mean, for the not so old and--
Just say I'm an old Smurf while you're at it!
POMPO NONO DZING
© Peyo
4

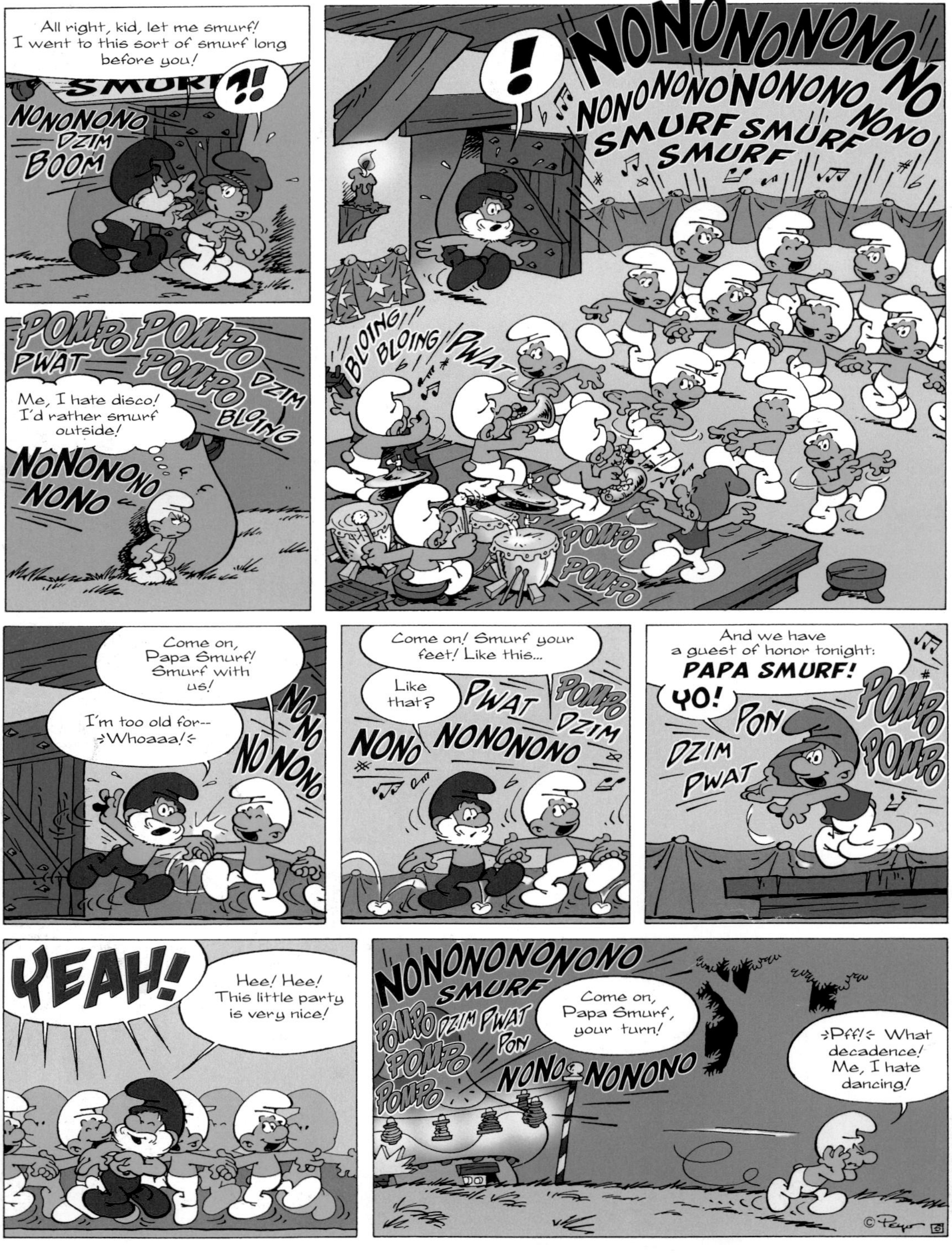

All right, kid, let me smurf! I went to this sort of smurf long before you!
SMURF
?!
NONONONO
DZIM
BOOM
!
NONONONONONO
NONONONONONONO NONO
SMURF SMURF
SMURF
POMPO POMPO
PWAT
POMPO
DZIM
BLOING
Me, I hate disco! I'd rather smurf outside!
NONONONO
NONO
BLOING
BLOING
PWAT
POMPO
POMPO
Come on, Papa Smurf! Smurf with us!
I'm too old for-- Whoaaa!
NONO
NONONO
Come on! Smurf your feet! Like this...
Like that?
PWAT
POMPO
DZIM
NONO
NONONONO
And we have a guest of honor tonight: PAPA SMURF!
YO!
PON
POMPO
POMPO
DZIM
PWAT
YEAH!
Hee! Hee! This little party is very nice!
NONONONONONO
SMURF
POMPO
DZIM
PWAT
PON
POMPO
POMPO
Come on, Papa Smurf, your turn!
NONO NONONO
Pff! What decadence! Me, I hate dancing!
© Peyo

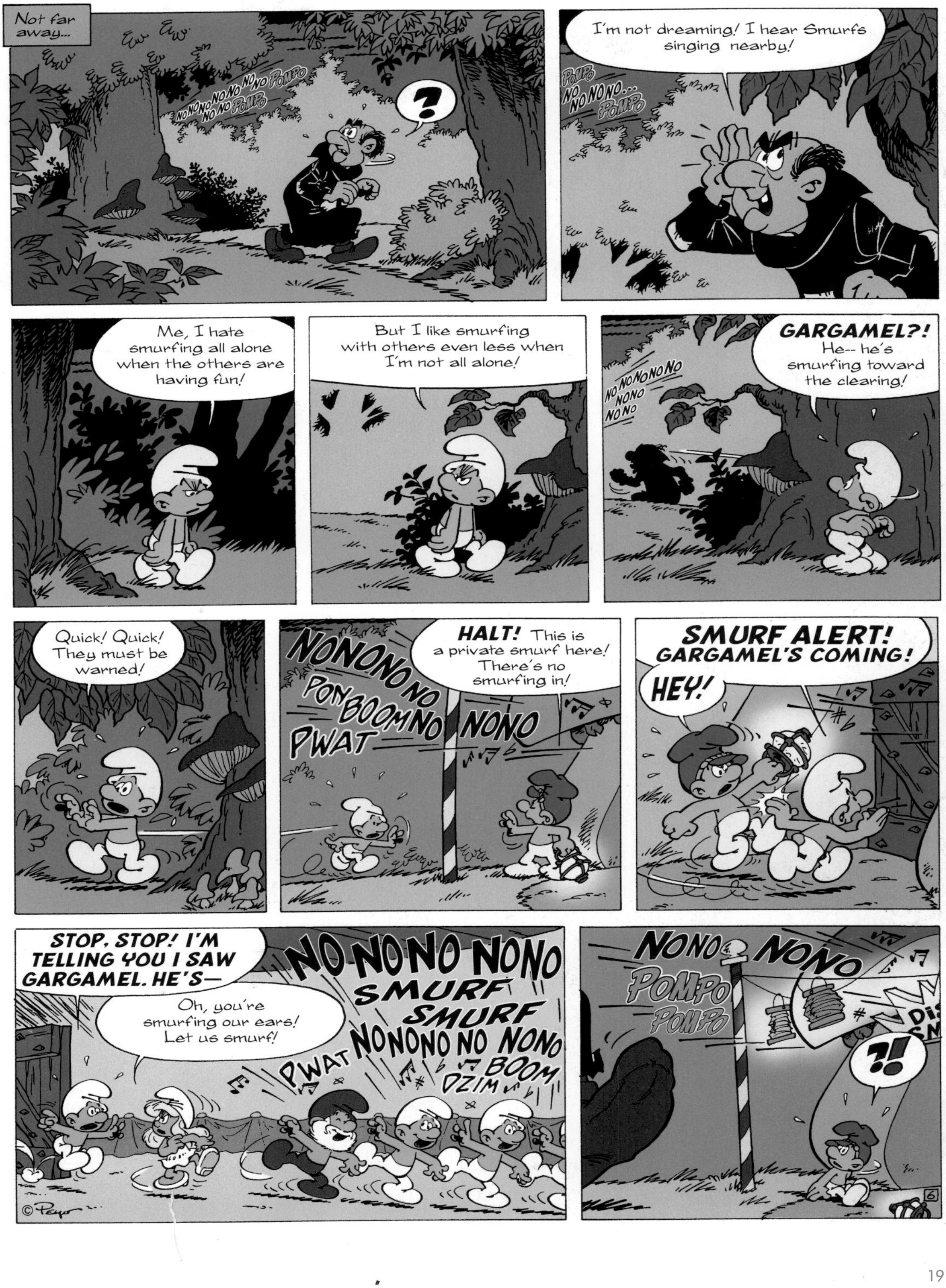
Not far away...
NONONONONONONONOPOMPO NONOPOMPO
?
POMPO NO NONONO... POMPO
I'm not dreaming! I hear Smurfs singing nearby!
Me, I hate smurfing all alone when the others are having fun!
But I like smurfing with others even less when I'm not all alone!
NONONONONO NONO NONO
GARGAMEL?! He-- he's smurfing toward the clearing!
Quick! Quick! They must be warned!
NONONO NO PONBOOMNO PWAT NONO
HALT! This is a private smurf here! There's no smurfing in!
SMURF ALERT! GARGAMEL'S COMING!
HEY!
STOP, STOP! I'M TELLING YOU I SAW GARGAMEL. HE'S—
NO NONO NONO SMURF SMURF NONONO NO NONO PWAT BOOM DZIM
Oh, you're smurfing our ears! Let us smurf!
© Peyo
NONO NONO POMPO POMPO
?!
6

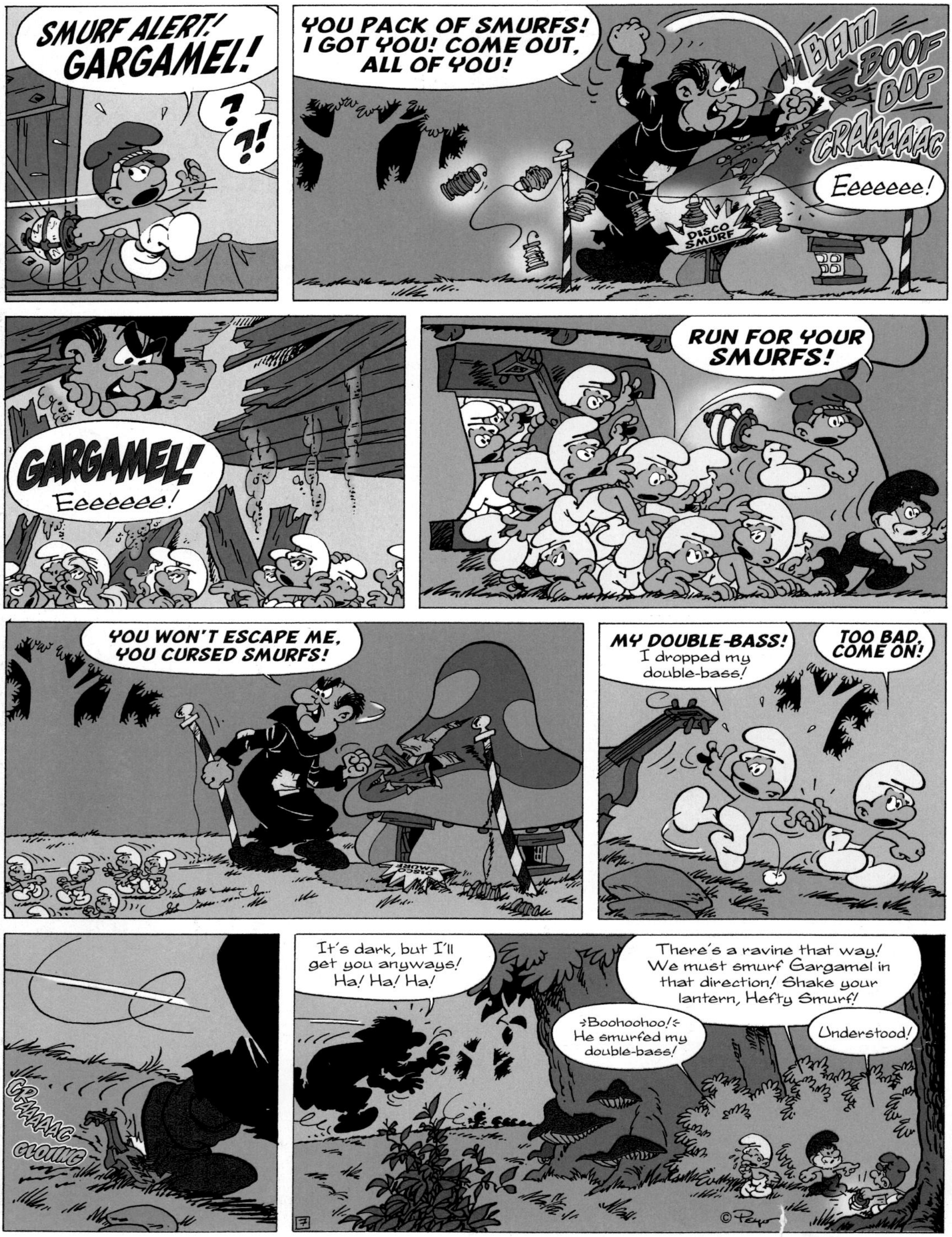
SMURF ALERT! GARGAMEL!
?
?!
YOU PACK OF SMURFS! I GOT YOU! COME OUT, ALL OF YOU!
BAM
BOOF
BOP
CRAAAAAC
Eeeeeee!
DISCO SMURF
GARGAMEL!
Eeeeeee!
RUN FOR YOUR SMURFS!
YOU WON'T ESCAPE ME, YOU CURSED SMURFS!
MY DOUBLE-BASS! I dropped my double-bass!
TOO BAD, COME ON!
CRAAAAC
CLOING
It's dark, but I'll get you anyways! Ha! Ha! Ha!
There's a ravine that way! We must smurf Gargamel in that direction! Shake your lantern, Hefty Smurf!
Boohoohoo! He smurfed my double-bass!
Understood!
7
© Peyo

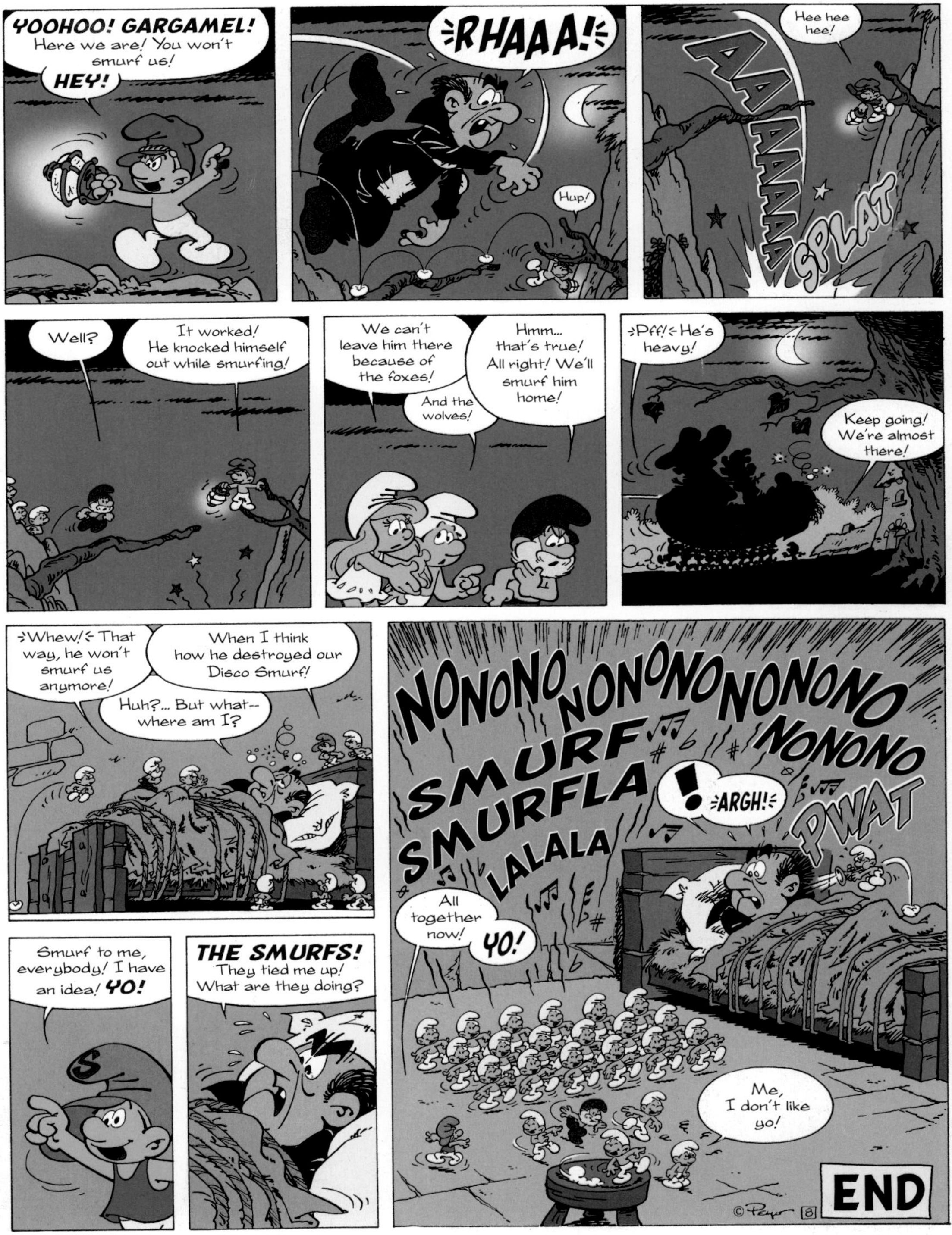
YOOHOO! GARGAMEL! Here we are! You won't smurf us!
HEY!
RHAAA!
Hup!
Hee hee hee!
AAAAAAAA
SPLAT
Well?
It worked! He knocked himself out while smurfing!
We can't leave him there because of the foxes!
And the wolves!
Hmm... that's true! All right! We'll smurf him home!
Pff! He's heavy!
Keep going! We're almost there!
Whew! That way, he won't smurf us anymore!
When I think how he destroyed our Disco Smurf!
Huh?... But what-- where am I?
Smurf to me, everybody! I have an idea! YO!
THE SMURFS! They tied me up! What are they doing?
NONONO NONONONONONO NONONO
SMURF SMURFLA LALALA
!
ARGH!
PWAT
All together now!
YO!
Me, I don't like yo!
END
© Peyo

THE OGRE AND THE SMURFS

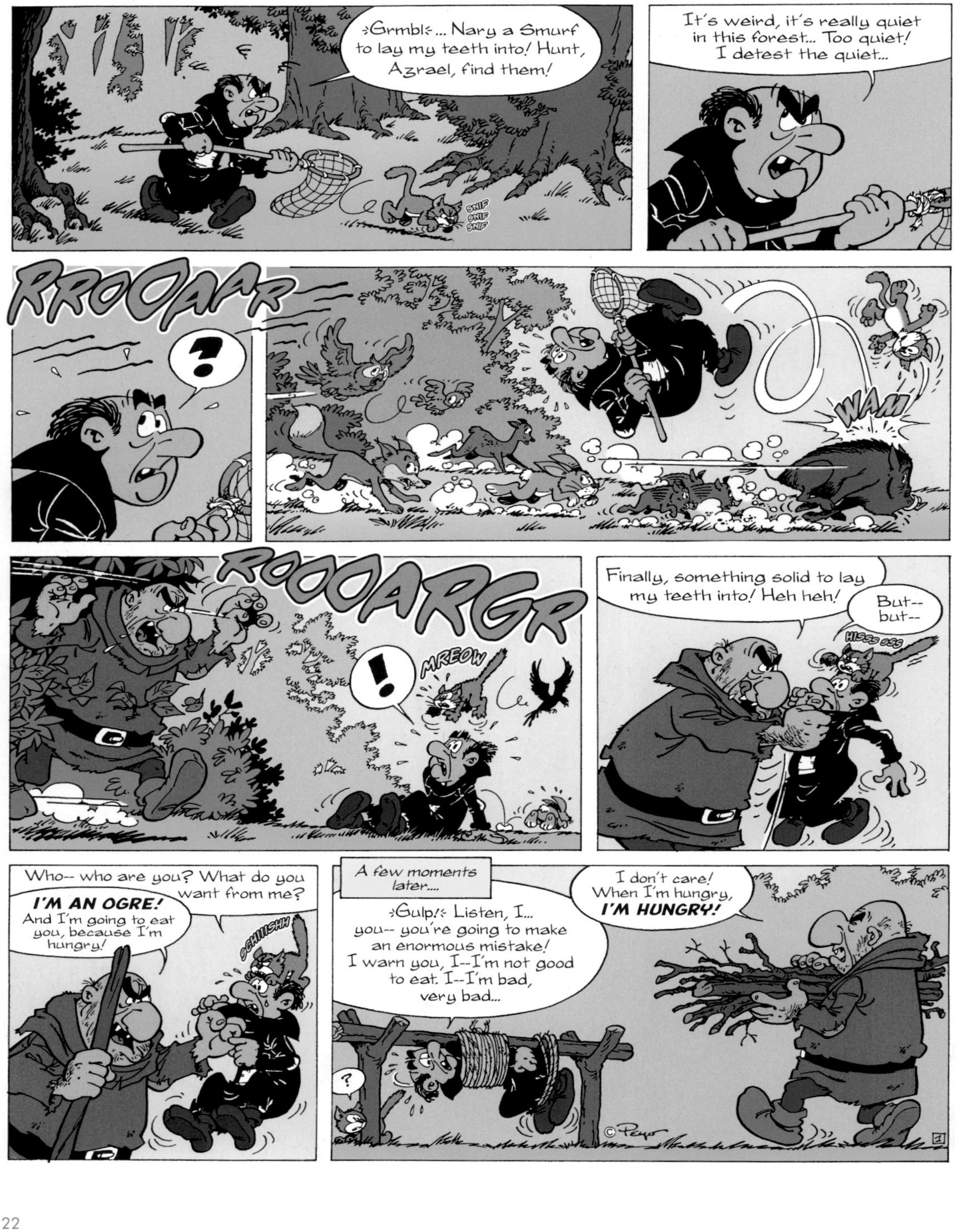

>Grmbl<... Nary a Smurf to lay my teeth into! Hunt, Azrael, find them!
SNIF SNIF SNIF
It's weird, it's really quiet in this forest... Too quiet! I detest the quiet...
RROOAAR
?
WAM
ROOOARGR
!
MREOW
Finally, something solid to lay my teeth into! Heh heh!
But-- but--
HISSSS SSS
Who-- who are you? What do you want from me?
I'M AN OGRE! And I'm going to eat you, because I'm hungry!
SCHHHSHH
A few moments later....
>Gulp!< Listen, I... you-- you're going to make an enormous mistake! I warn you, I--I'm not good to eat. I--I'm bad, very bad...
?
I don't care! When I'm hungry, **I'M HUNGRY!**
© Peyo
1

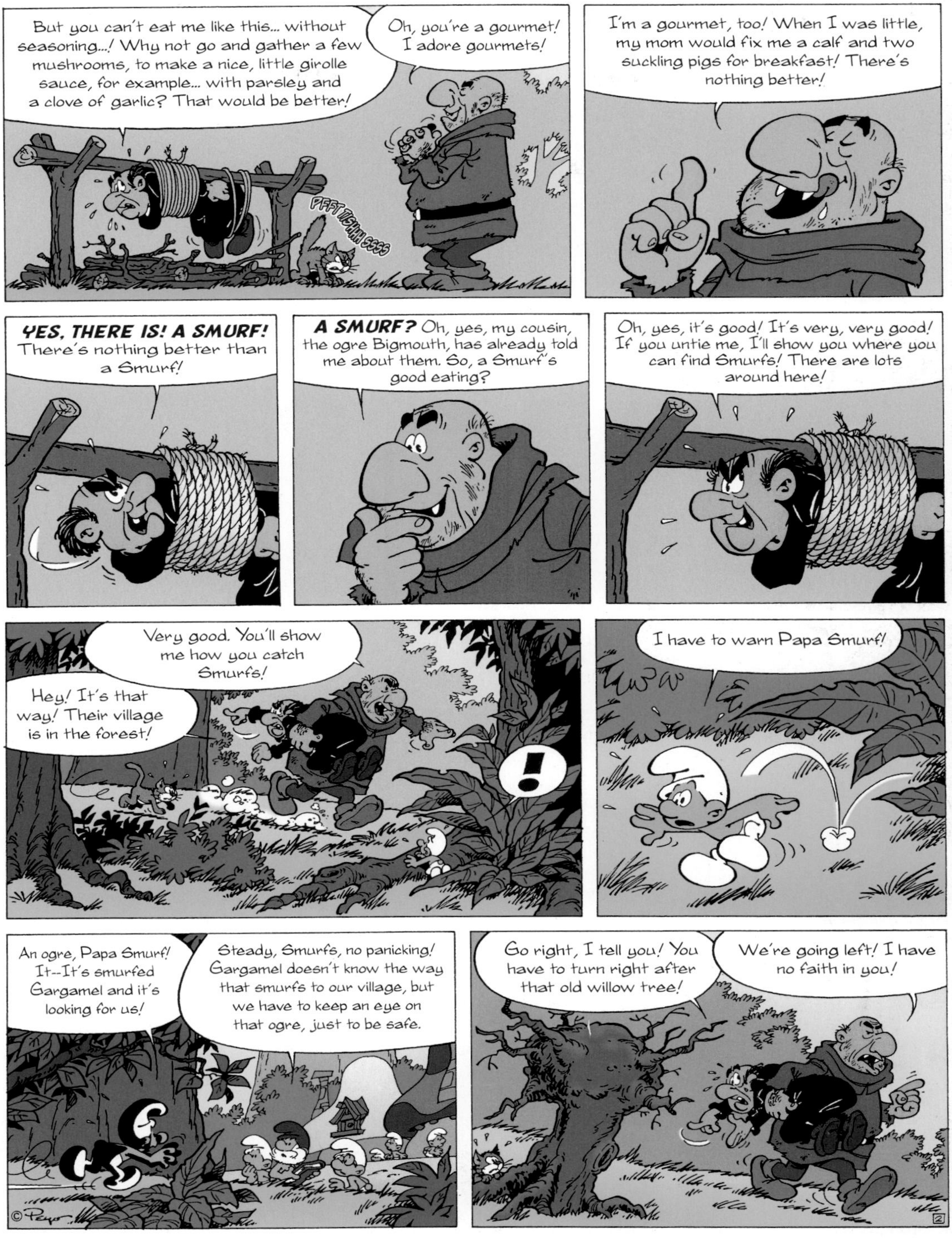
But you can't eat me like this... without seasoning...! Why not go and gather a few mushrooms, to make a nice, little girolle sauce, for example... with parsley and a clove of garlic? That would be better!
Oh, you're a gourmet! I adore gourmets!
PFFT TISHHH SSSS
I'm a gourmet, too! When I was little, my mom would fix me a calf and two suckling pigs for breakfast! There's nothing better!
YES, THERE IS! A SMURF! There's nothing better than a Smurf!
A SMURF? Oh, yes, my cousin, the ogre Bigmouth, has already told me about them. So, a Smurf's good eating?
Oh, yes, it's good! It's very, very good! If you untie me, I'll show you where you can find Smurfs! There are lots around here!
Very good. You'll show me how you catch Smurfs!
Hey! It's that way! Their village is in the forest!
!
I have to warn Papa Smurf!
An ogre, Papa Smurf! It--It's smurfed Gargamel and it's looking for us!
Steady, Smurfs, no panicking! Gargamel doesn't know the way that smurfs to our village, but we have to keep an eye on that ogre, just to be safe.
Go right, I tell you! You have to turn right after that old willow tree!
We're going left! I have no faith in you!
© Peyo
2

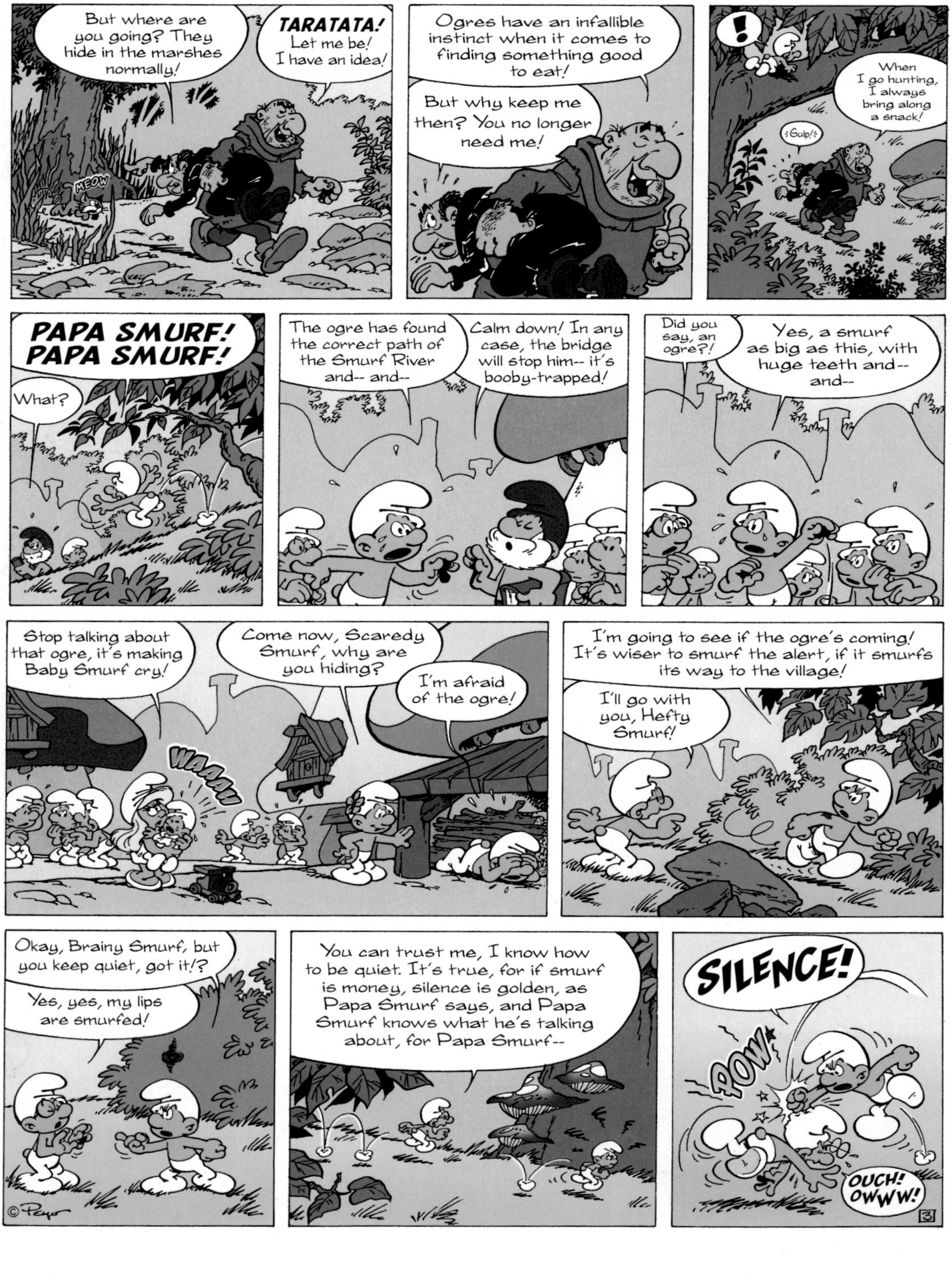

But where are you going? They hide in the marshes normally!
MEOW
TARATATA! Let me be! I have an idea!
Ogres have an infallible instinct when it comes to finding something good to eat!
But why keep me then? You no longer need me!
!
Gulp!
When I go hunting, I always bring along a snack!
PAPA SMURF! PAPA SMURF!
What?
The ogre has found the correct path of the Smurf River and-- and--
Calm down! In any case, the bridge will stop him-- it's booby-trapped!
Did you say, an ogre?!
Yes, a smurf as big as this, with huge teeth and-- and--
Stop talking about that ogre, it's making Baby Smurf cry!
WAAAH
Come now, Scaredy Smurf, why are you hiding?
I'm afraid of the ogre!
I'm going to see if the ogre's coming! It's wiser to smurf the alert, if it smurfs its way to the village!
I'll go with you, Hefty Smurf!
Okay, Brainy Smurf, but you keep quiet, got it!?
Yes, yes, my lips are smurfed!
You can trust me, I know how to be quiet. It's true, for if smurf is money, silence is golden, as Papa Smurf says, and Papa Smurf knows what he's talking about, for Papa Smurf--
SILENCE!
POW
OUCH! OWWW!
© Peyo
3

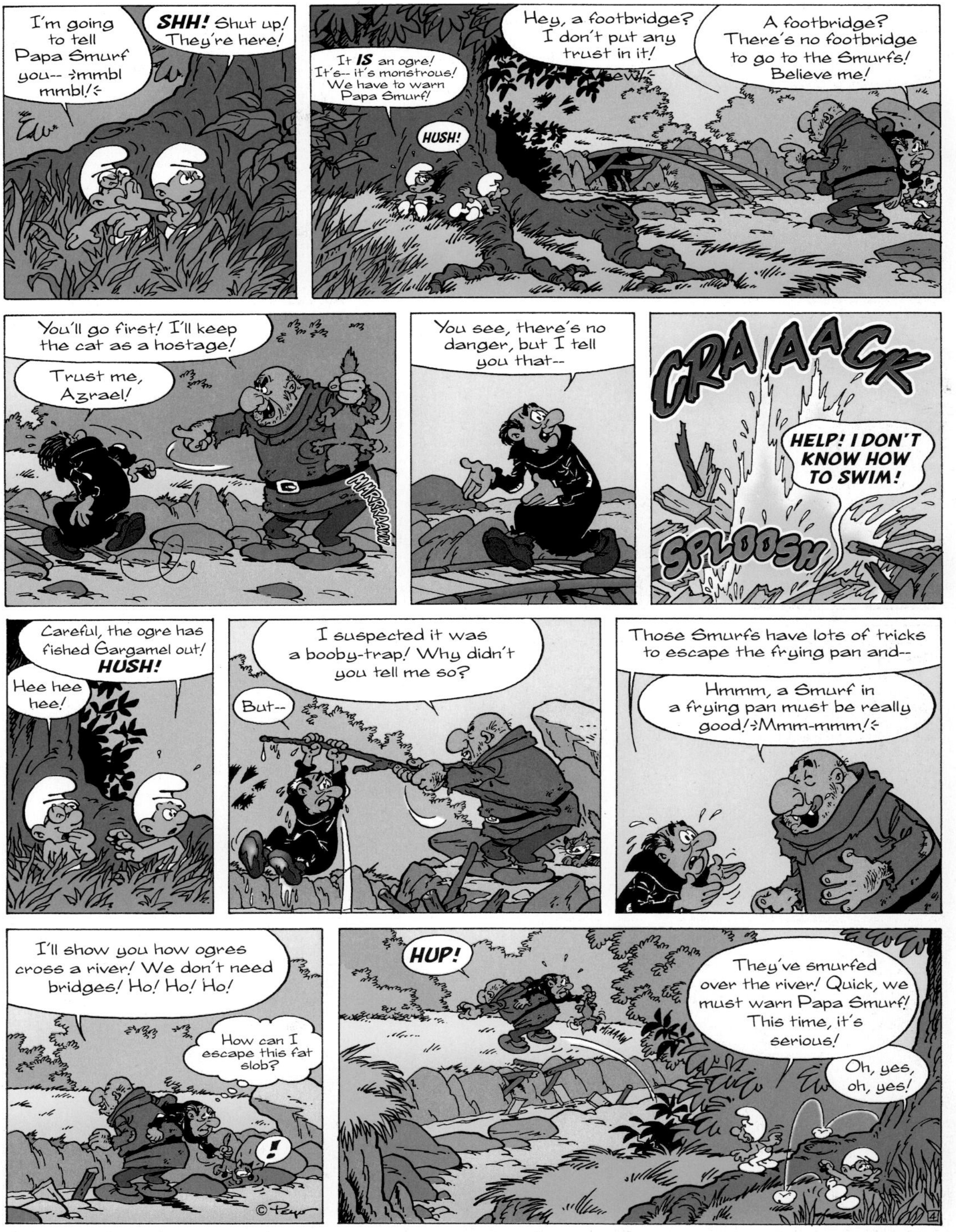

I'm going to tell Papa Smurf you-- ⪼mmbl mmbl!⪻
SHH! Shut up! They're here!
It IS an ogre! It's-- it's monstrous! We have to warn Papa Smurf!
HUSH!
Hey, a footbridge? I don't put any trust in it!
A footbridge? There's no footbridge to go to the Smurfs! Believe me!
You'll go first! I'll keep the cat as a hostage!
Trust me, Azrael!
MRRRAAAW
You see, there's no danger, but I tell you that--
CRAAACK
HELP! I DON'T KNOW HOW TO SWIM!
SPLOOSH
Careful, the ogre has fished Gargamel out!
HUSH!
Hee hee hee!
I suspected it was a booby-trap! Why didn't you tell me so?
But--
Those Smurfs have lots of tricks to escape the frying pan and--
Hmmm, a Smurf in a frying pan must be really good! ⪼Mmm-mmm!⪻
I'll show you how ogres cross a river! We don't need bridges! Ho! Ho! Ho!
How can I escape this fat slob?
!
© Peyo
HUP!
They've smurfed over the river! Quick, we must warn Papa Smurf! This time, it's serious!
Oh, yes, oh, yes!
4

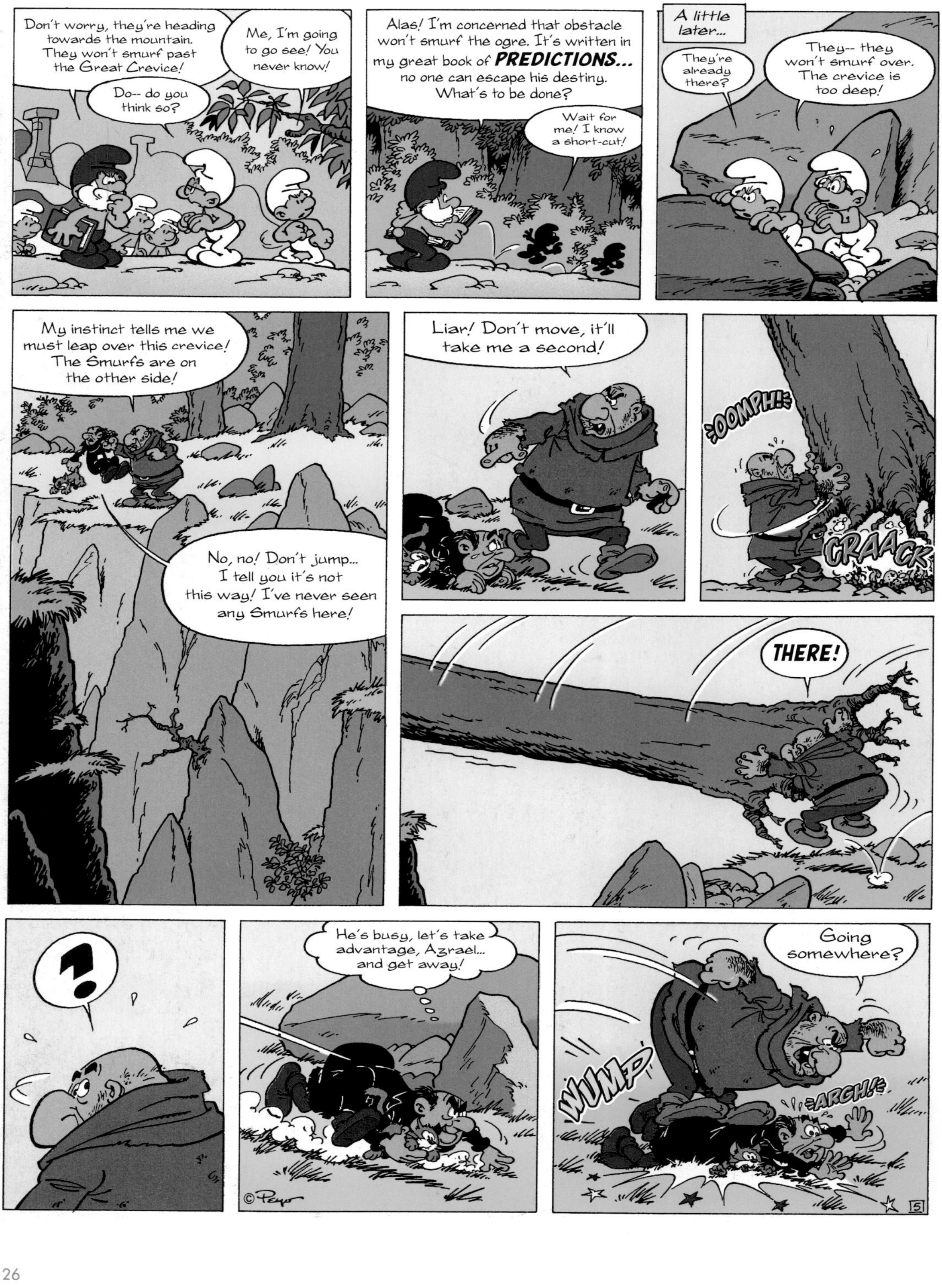
Don't worry, they're heading towards the mountain. They won't smurf past the Great Crevice!
Do-- do you think so?
Me, I'm going to go see! You never know!
Alas! I'm concerned that obstacle won't smurf the ogre. It's written in my great book of PREDICTIONS... no one can escape his destiny. What's to be done?
Wait for me! I know a short-cut!
A little later...
They're already there?
They-- they won't smurf over. The crevice is too deep!
My instinct tells me we must leap over this crevice! The Smurfs are on the other side!
No, no! Don't jump... I tell you it's not this way! I've never seen any Smurfs here!
Liar! Don't move, it'll take me a second!
OOMPH!
CRAACK
THERE!
?
He's busy, let's take advantage, Azrael... and get away!
© Peyo
Going somewhere?
WUMP
ARGH!
5

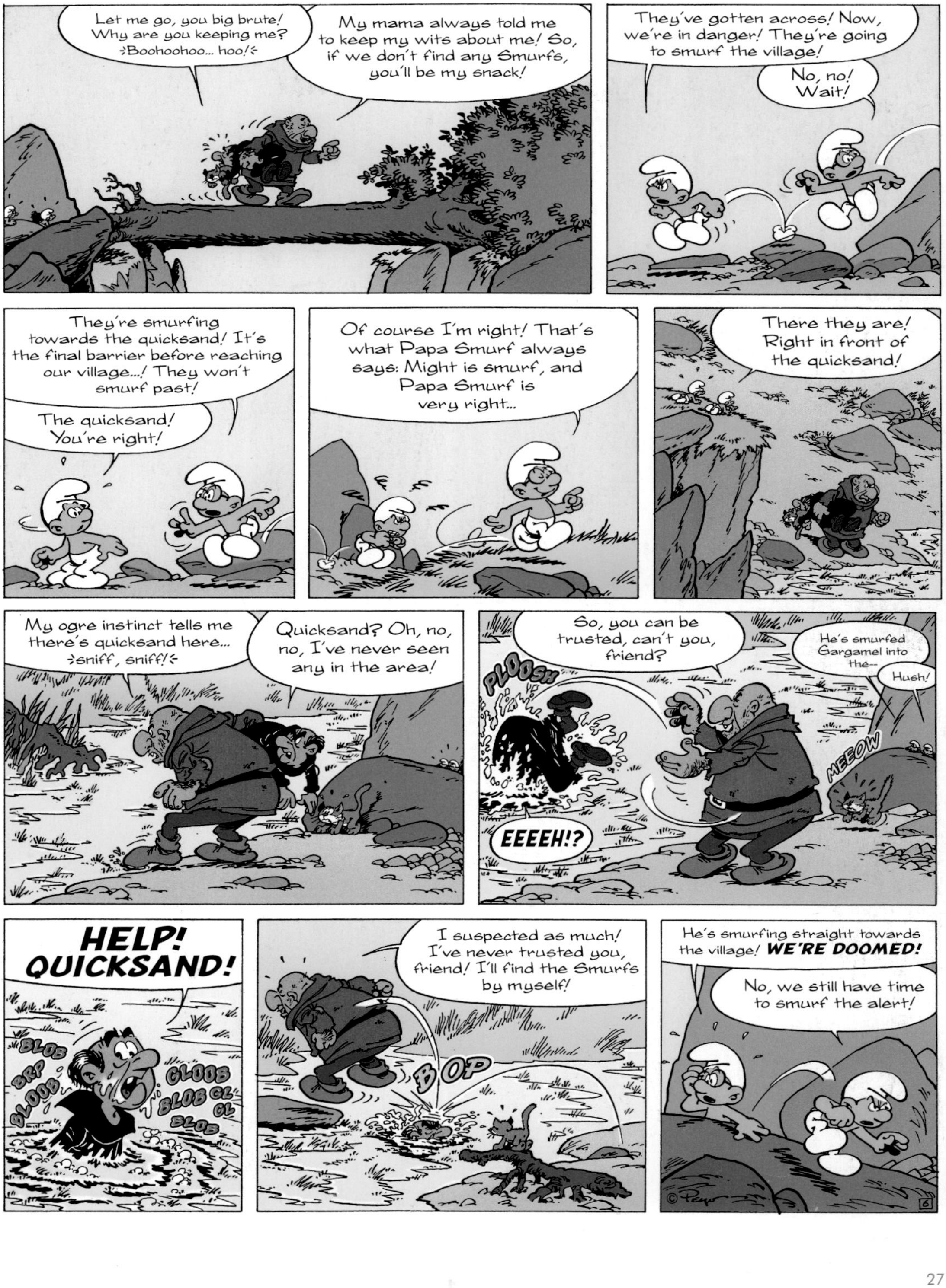
Let me go, you big brute! Why are you keeping me? -Boohoohoo... hoo!-
My mama always told me to keep my wits about me! So, if we don't find any Smurfs, you'll be my snack!
They've gotten across! Now, we're in danger! They're going to smurf the village!
No, no! Wait!
They're smurfing towards the quicksand! It's the final barrier before reaching our village...! They won't smurf past!
The quicksand! You're right!
Of course I'm right! That's what Papa Smurf always says: Might is smurf, and Papa Smurf is very right...
There they are! Right in front of the quicksand!
My ogre instinct tells me there's quicksand here... -sniff, sniff!-
Quicksand? Oh, no, no, I've never seen any in the area!
So, you can be trusted, can't you, friend?
He's smurfed Gargamel into the--
Hush!
PLOOSH
MEEOW
EEEEH!?
HELP! QUICKSAND!
BLOB
BRP
BLOOB
GLOOB
BLOB GL
GL
BLOB
I suspected as much! I've never trusted you, friend! I'll find the Smurfs by myself!
BOP
He's smurfing straight towards the village! WE'RE DOOMED!
No, we still have time to smurf the alert!
© Peyo
6

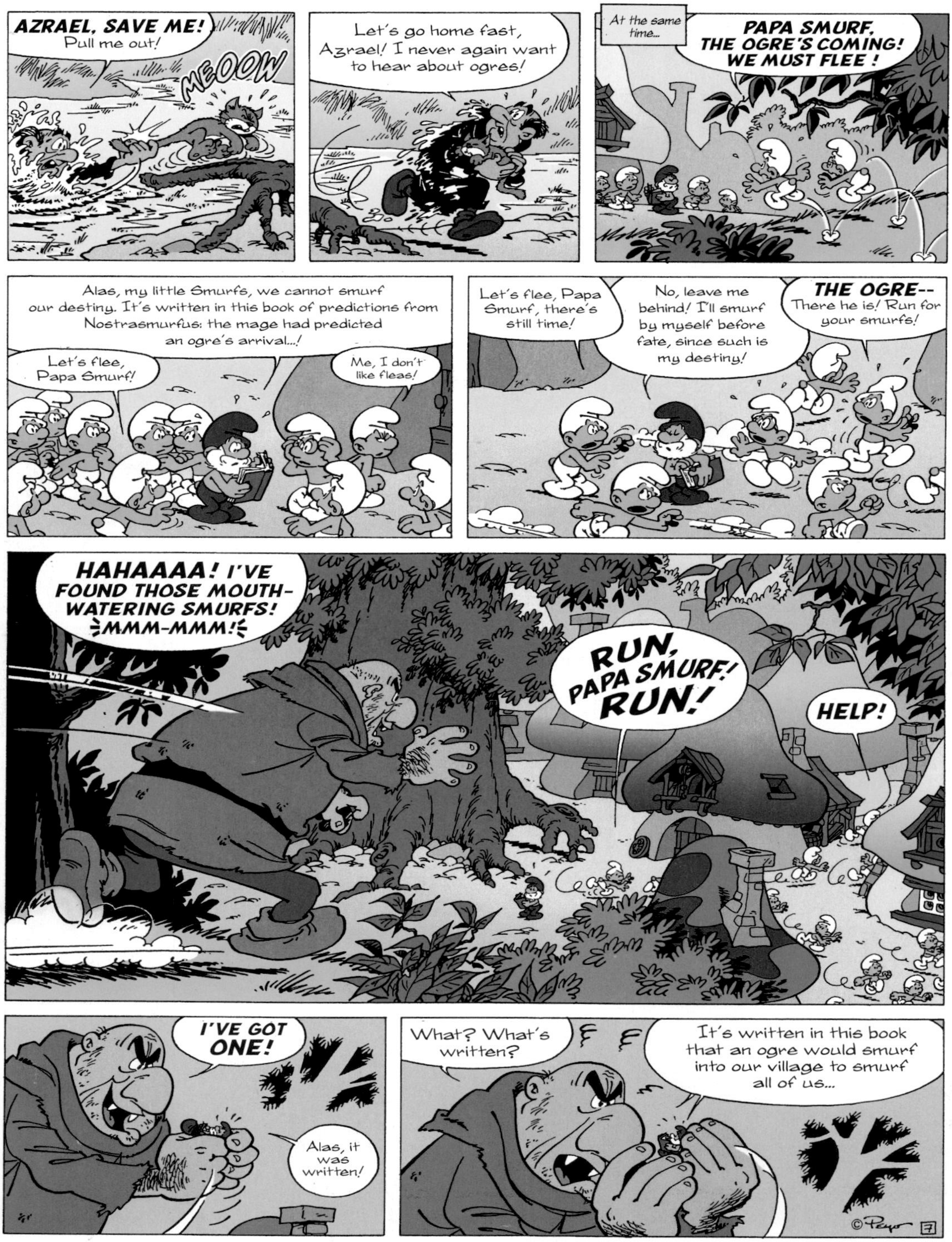
AZRAEL, SAVE ME! Pull me out!
MEOOW
Let's go home fast, Azrael! I never again want to hear about ogres!
At the same time...
PAPA SMURF, THE OGRE'S COMING! WE MUST FLEE !
Alas, my little Smurfs, we cannot smurf our destiny. It's written in this book of predictions from Nostrasmurfus: the mage had predicted an ogre's arrival...!
Let's flee, Papa Smurf!
Me, I don't like fleas!
Let's flee, Papa Smurf, there's still time!
No, leave me behind! I'll smurf by myself before fate, since such is my destiny!
THE OGRE-- There he is! Run for your smurfs!
HAHAAAA! I'VE FOUND THOSE MOUTH-WATERING SMURFS! MMM-MMM!
RUN, PAPA SMURF! RUN!
HELP!
I'VE GOT ONE!
Alas, it was written!
What? What's written?
It's written in this book that an ogre would smurf into our village to smurf all of us...
© Peyo
7

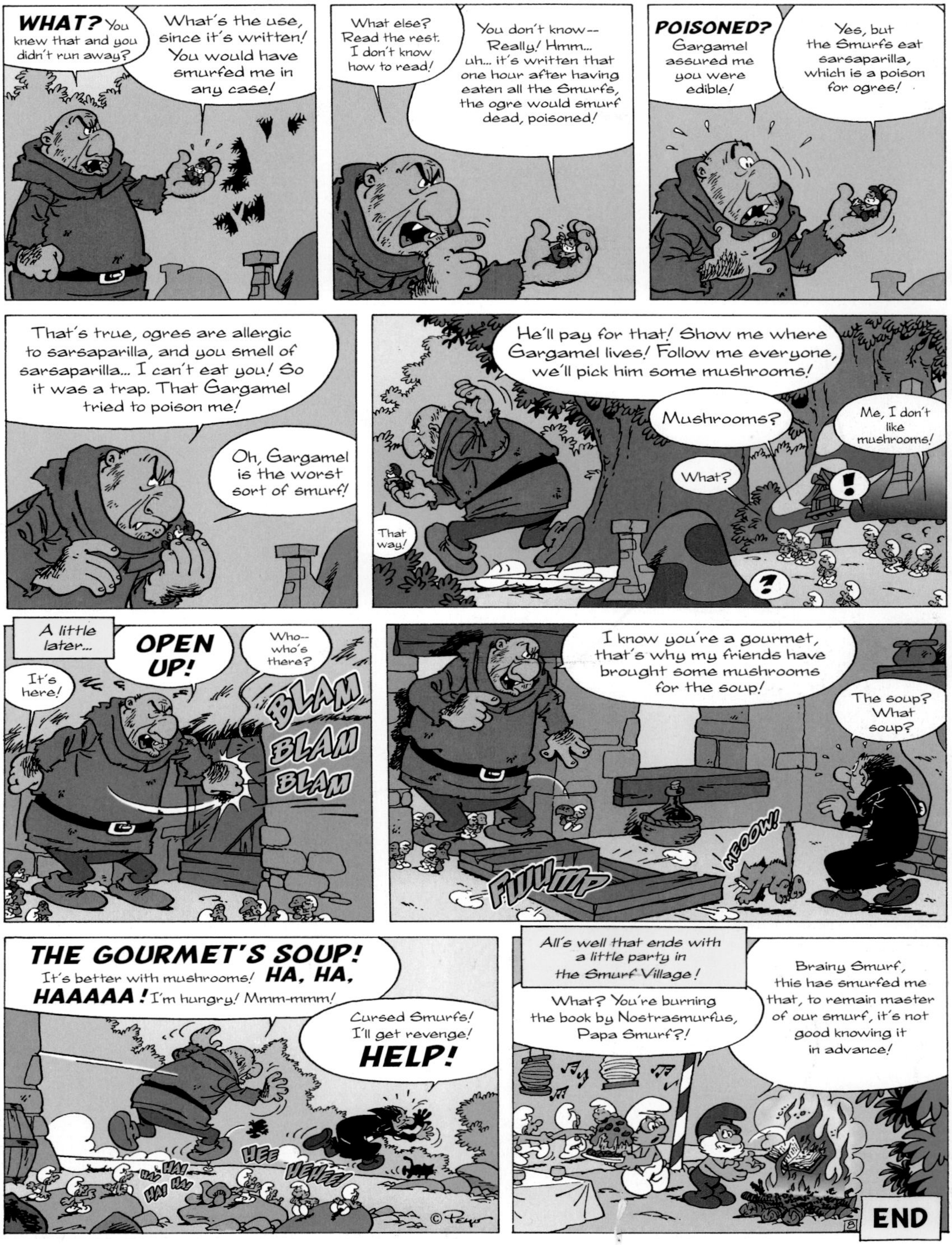
WHAT? You knew that and you didn't run away?
What's the use, since it's written! You would have smurfed me in any case!
What else? Read the rest. I don't know how to read!
You don't know-- Really! Hmm... uh... it's written that one hour after having eaten all the Smurfs, the ogre would smurf dead, poisoned!
POISONED? Gargamel assured me you were edible!
Yes, but the Smurfs eat sarsaparilla, which is a poison for ogres!
That's true, ogres are allergic to sarsaparilla, and you smell of sarsaparilla... I can't eat you! So it was a trap. That Gargamel tried to poison me!
Oh, Gargamel is the worst sort of smurf!
He'll pay for that! Show me where Gargamel lives! Follow me everyone, we'll pick him some mushrooms!
Mushrooms?
Me, I don't like mushrooms!
What?
That way!
A little later...
It's here!
OPEN UP!
Who-- who's there?
BLAM BLAM BLAM
I know you're a gourmet, that's why my friends have brought some mushrooms for the soup!
The soup? What soup?
FWUUMP
MEOOW!
THE GOURMET'S SOUP! It's better with mushrooms! HA, HA, HAAAAA! I'm hungry! Mmm-mmm!
Cursed Smurfs! I'll get revenge! HELP!
HEE HEHEE!
HA! HA! HA! HA!
© Peyo
All's well that ends with a little party in the Smurf Village!
What? You're burning the book by Nostrasmurfus, Papa Smurf?!
Brainy Smurf, this has smurfed me that, to remain master of our smurf, it's not good knowing it in advance!
END

GARGAMEL'S TWIN BROTHER

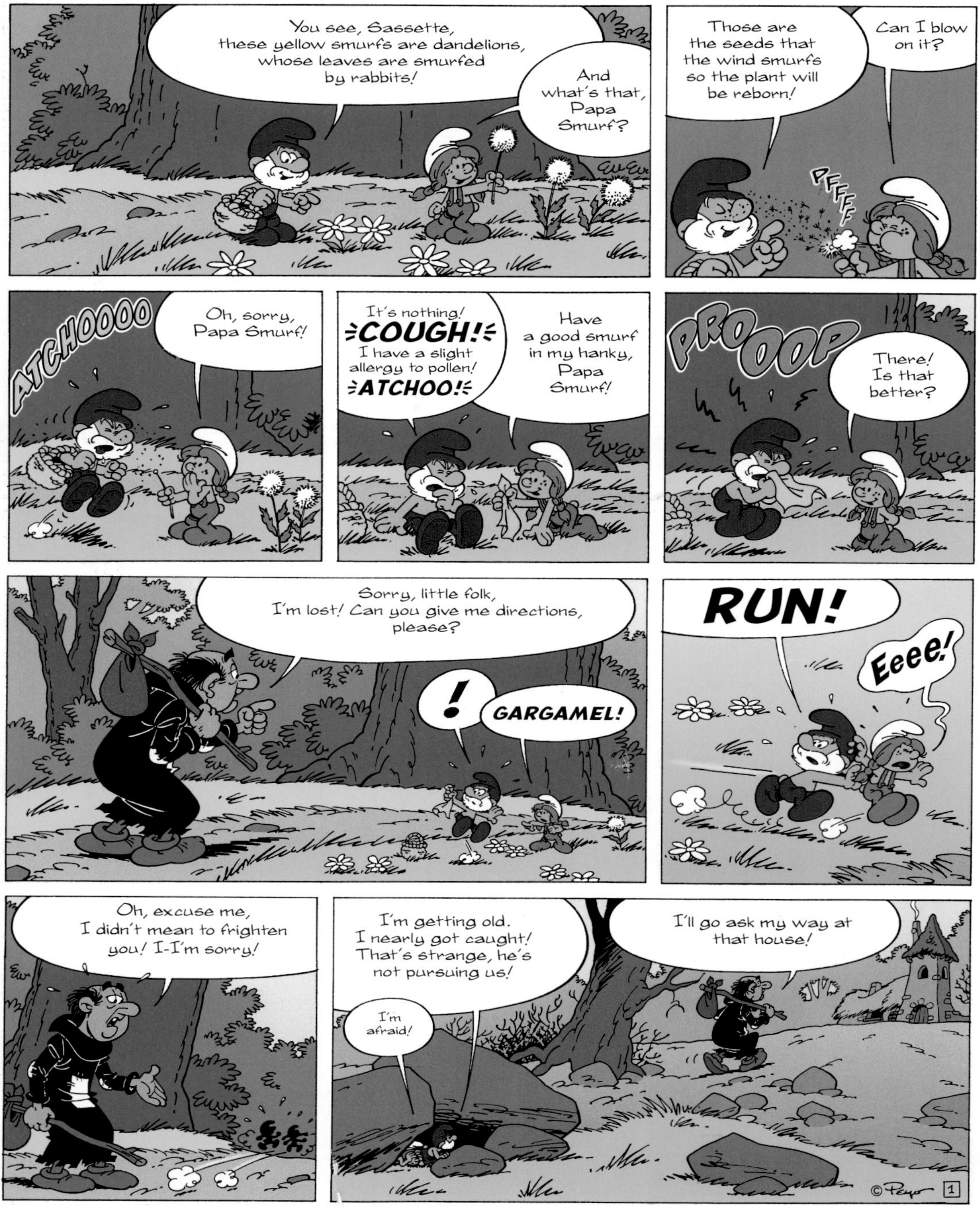
You see, Sassette, these yellow smurfs are dandelions, whose leaves are smurfed by rabbits!
And what's that, Papa Smurf?
Those are the seeds that the wind smurfs so the plant will be reborn!
Can I blow on it?
PFFFF
ATCHOOOO
Oh, sorry, Papa Smurf!
It's nothing! COUGH! I have a slight allergy to pollen! ATCHOO!
Have a good smurf in my hanky, Papa Smurf!
PROOOOP
There! Is that better?
Sorry, little folk, I'm lost! Can you give me directions, please?
!
GARGAMEL!
RUN!
Eeee!
Oh, excuse me, I didn't mean to frighten you! I-I'm sorry!
I'm getting old. I nearly got caught! That's strange, he's not pursuing us!
I'm afraid!
I'll go ask my way at that house!
© Peyo
1

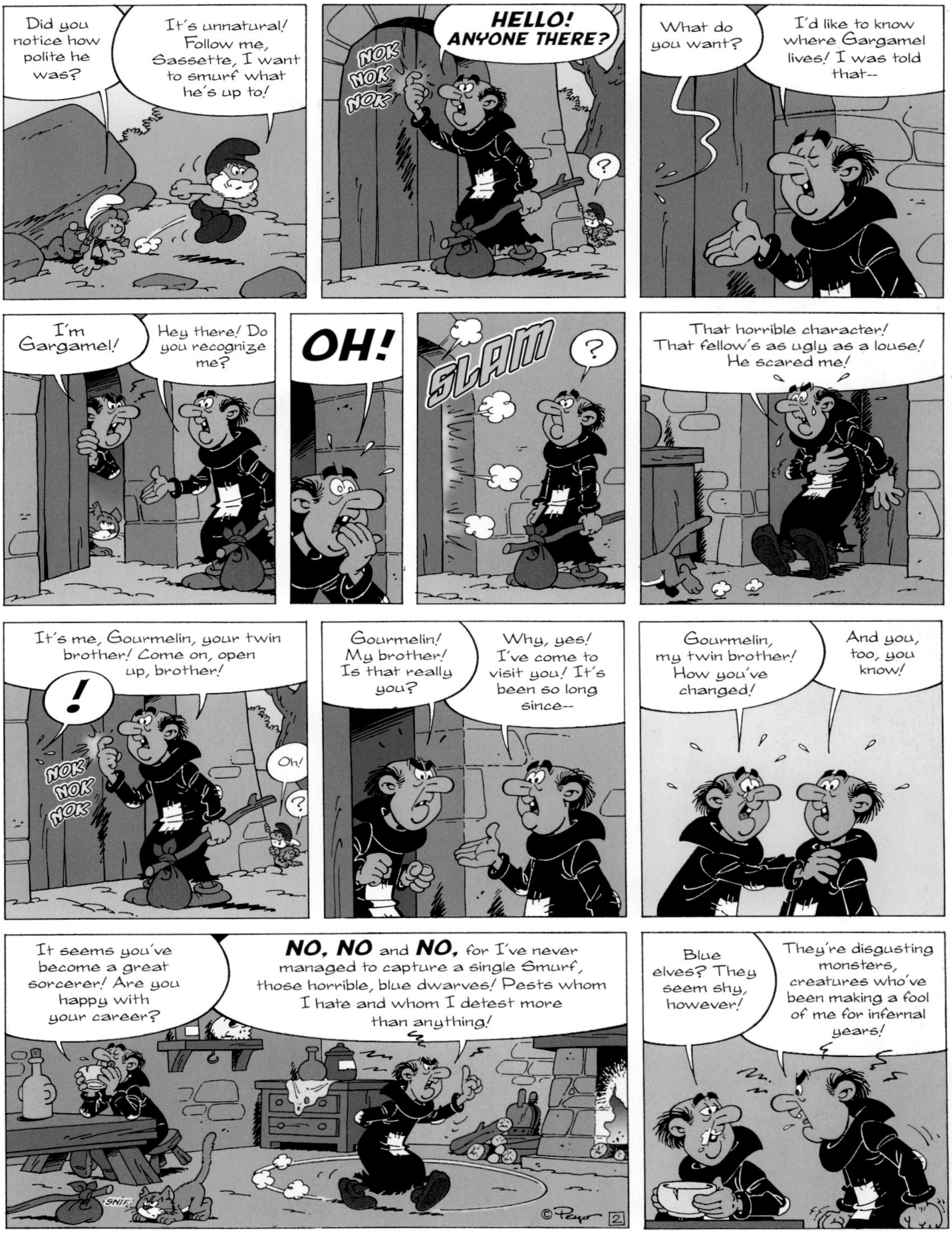

Did you notice how polite he was?
It's unnatural! Follow me, Sassette, I want to smurf what he's up to!
NOK NOK NOK
HELLO! ANYONE THERE?
?
What do you want?
I'd like to know where Gargamel lives! I was told that--
I'm Gargamel!
Hey there! Do you recognize me?
OH!
SLAM
?
That horrible character! That fellow's as ugly as a louse! He scared me!
It's me, Gourmelin, your twin brother! Come on, open up, brother!
!
NOK NOK NOK
Oh!
?
Gourmelin! My brother! Is that really you?
Why, yes! I've come to visit you! It's been so long since--
Gourmelin, my twin brother! How you've changed!
And you, too, you know!
It seems you've become a great sorcerer! Are you happy with your career?
NO, NO and NO, for I've never managed to capture a single Smurf, those horrible, blue dwarves! Pests whom I hate and whom I detest more than anything!
SNIF
© Peyo 2
Blue elves? They seem shy, however!
They're disgusting monsters, creatures who've been making a fool of me for infernal years!

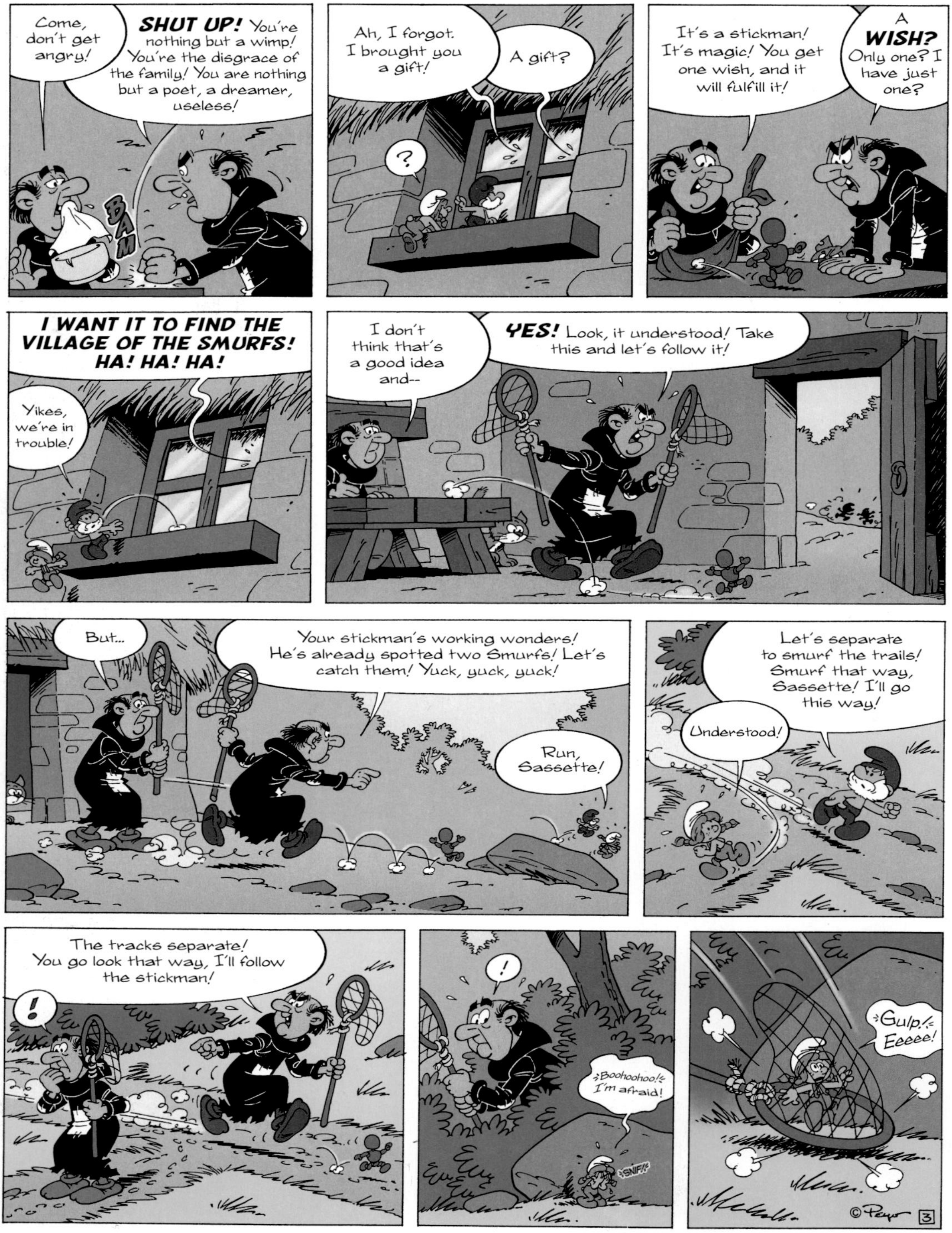

Come, don't get angry!
SHUT UP! You're nothing but a wimp! You're the disgrace of the family! You are nothing but a poet, a dreamer, useless!
BAM
Ah, I forgot. I brought you a gift!
A gift?
?
It's a stickman! It's magic! You get one wish, and it will fulfill it!
A WISH? Only one? I have just one?
I WANT IT TO FIND THE VILLAGE OF THE SMURFS! HA! HA! HA!
Yikes, we're in trouble!
I don't think that's a good idea and--
YES! Look, it understood! Take this and let's follow it!
But...
Your stickman's working wonders! He's already spotted two Smurfs! Let's catch them! Yuck, yuck, yuck!
Run, Sassette!
Let's separate to smurf the trails! Smurf that way, Sassette! I'll go this way!
Understood!
The tracks separate! You go look that way, I'll follow the stickman!
!
!
Boohoohoo! I'm afraid!
SNIF!
Gulp! Eeeee!
© Peyo 3

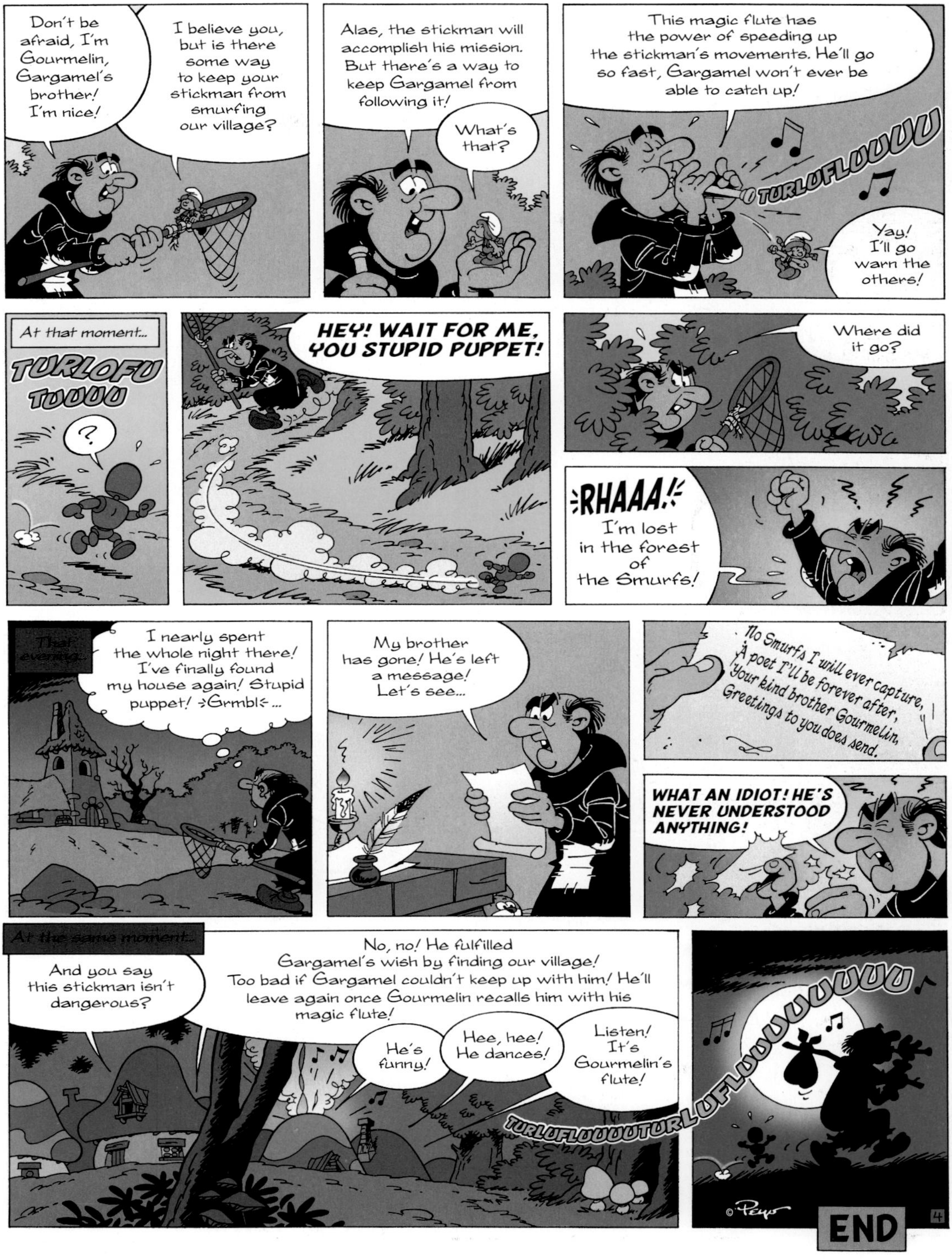
Don't be afraid, I'm Gourmelin, Gargamel's brother! I'm nice!
I believe you, but is there some way to keep your stickman from smurfing our village?
Alas, the stickman will accomplish his mission. But there's a way to keep Gargamel from following it!
What's that?
This magic flute has the power of speeding up the stickman's movements. He'll go so fast, Gargamel won't ever be able to catch up!
TURLUFLUUUU
Yay! I'll go warn the others!
At that moment...
TURLOFU TUUUU
?
HEY! WAIT FOR ME, YOU STUPID PUPPET!
Where did it go?
RHAAA! I'm lost in the forest of the Smurfs!
That evening...
I nearly spent the whole night there! I've finally found my house again! Stupid puppet! >Grmbl< ...
My brother has gone! He's left a message! Let's see...
No Smurfs I will ever capture, A poet I'll be forever after, Your kind brother Gourmelin, Greetings to you does send.
WHAT AN IDIOT! HE'S NEVER UNDERSTOOD ANYTHING!
At the same moment...
And you say this stickman isn't dangerous?
No, no! He fulfilled Gargamel's wish by finding our village! Too bad if Gargamel couldn't keep up with him! He'll leave again once Gourmelin recalls him with his magic flute!
He's funny!
Hee, hee! He dances!
Listen! It's Gourmelin's flute!
TURLUFLUUUUTURLUFLUUUUUUUUU
© Peyo
4
END

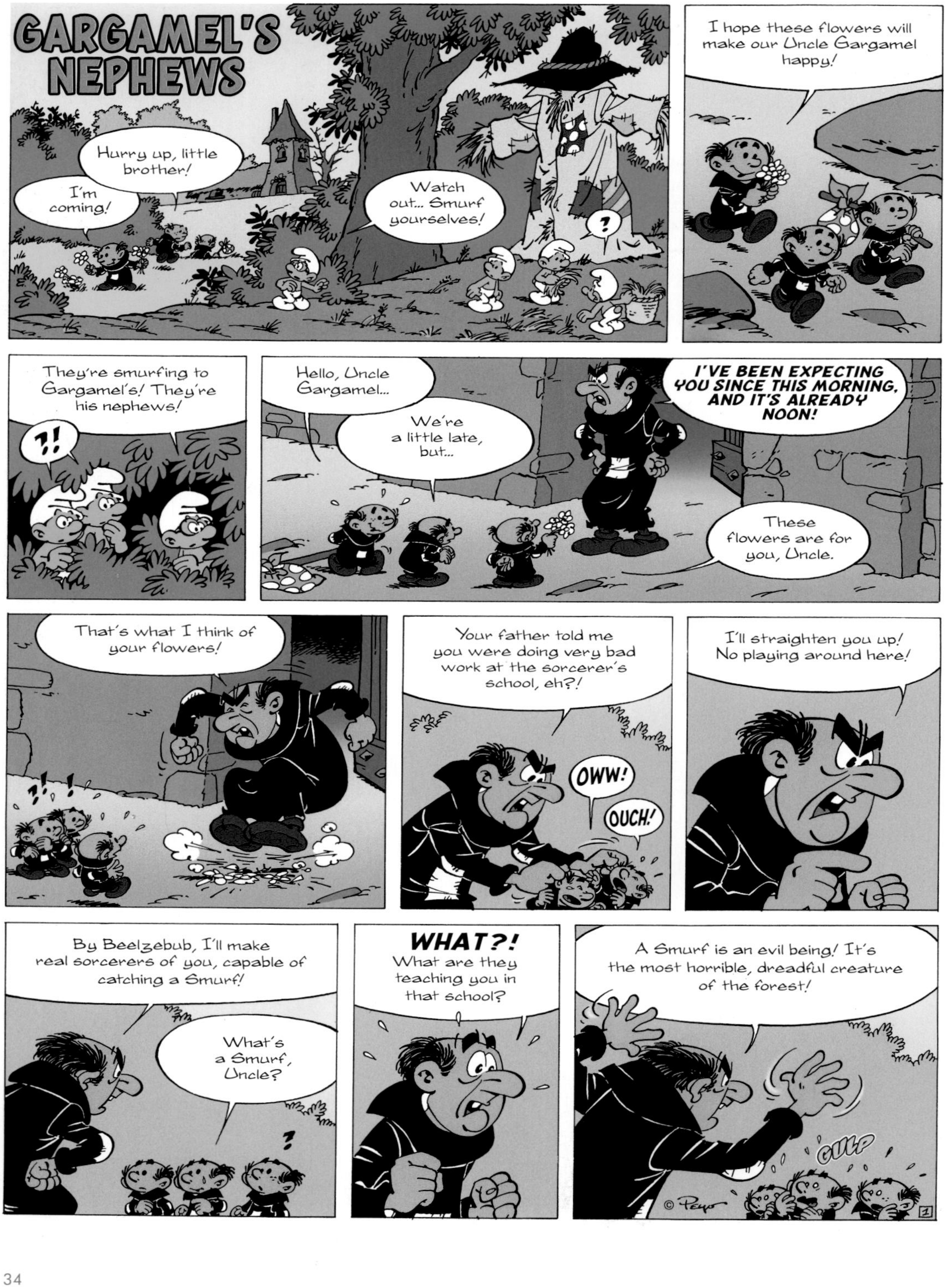

GARGAMEL'S NEPHEWS
Hurry up, little brother!
I'm coming!
Watch out... Smurf yourselves!
?
I hope these flowers will make our Uncle Gargamel happy!
They're smurfing to Gargamel's! They're his nephews!
?!
Hello, Uncle Gargamel...
We're a little late, but...
I'VE BEEN EXPECTING YOU SINCE THIS MORNING, AND IT'S ALREADY NOON!
These flowers are for you, Uncle.
That's what I think of your flowers!
Your father told me you were doing very bad work at the sorcerer's school, eh?!
OWW!
OUCH!
I'll straighten you up! No playing around here!
By Beelzebub, I'll make real sorcerers of you, capable of catching a Smurf!
What's a Smurf, Uncle?
?
WHAT?!
What are they teaching you in that school?
A Smurf is an evil being! It's the most horrible, dreadful creature of the forest!
GULP
© Peyo
1

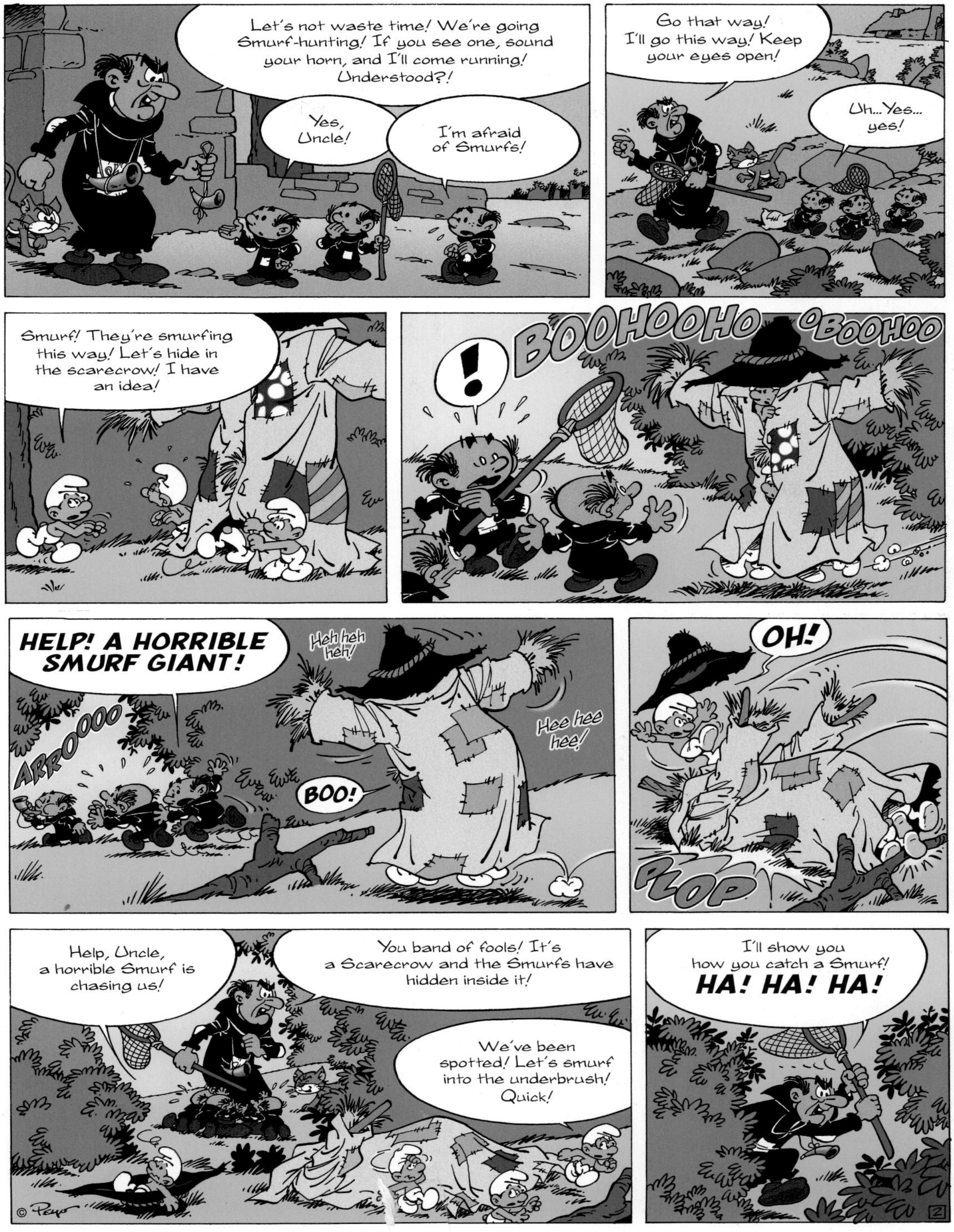

Let's not waste time! We're going Smurf-hunting! If you see one, sound your horn, and I'll come running! Understood?!
Yes, Uncle!
I'm afraid of Smurfs!
Go that way! I'll go this way! Keep your eyes open!
Uh... Yes... yes!
Smurf! They're smurfing this way! Let's hide in the scarecrow! I have an idea!
!
BOOHOOHO OBOOHOO
HELP! A HORRIBLE SMURF GIANT!
Heh heh heh!
ARROOOO
Hee hee hee!
BOO!
OH!
PLOP
Help, Uncle, a horrible Smurf is chasing us!
You band of fools! It's a Scarecrow and the Smurfs have hidden inside it!
We've been spotted! Let's smurf into the underbrush! Quick!
© Peyo
I'll show you how you catch a Smurf! HA! HA! HA!
2

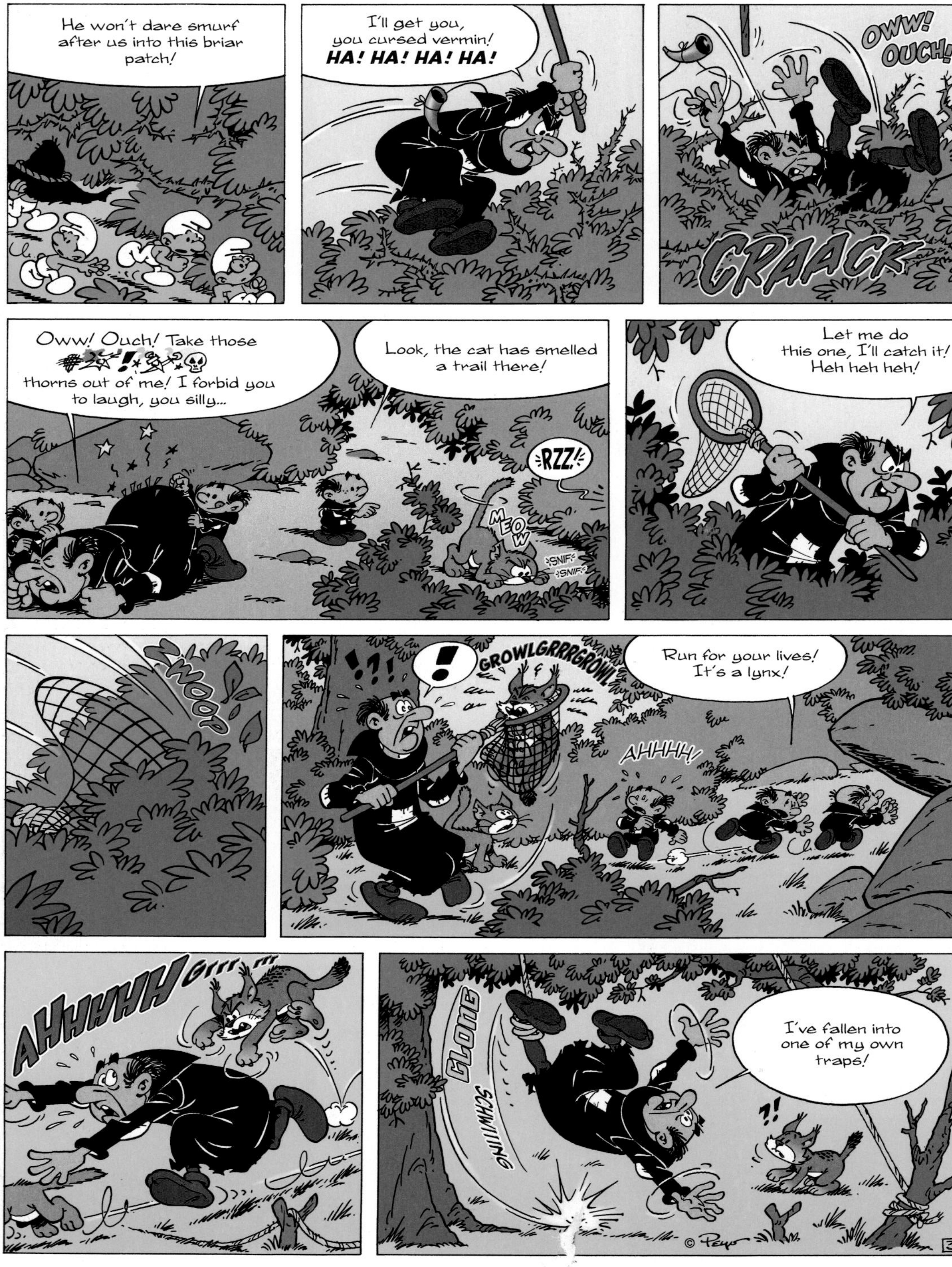
He won't dare smurf after us into this briar patch!
I'll get you, you cursed vermin! HA! HA! HA! HA!
OWW! OUCH!
CRAACK
Oww! Ouch! Take those thorns out of me! I forbid you to laugh, you silly...
Look, the cat has smelled a trail there!
RZZ!
MEOW
SNIF SNIF
Let me do this one, I'll catch it! Heh heh heh!
ZWOOP
!?!
!
GROWLGRRRGROWL
Run for your lives! It's a lynx!
AHHHH!
AHHHHH
Grrr rrr
CLONG
SCHWIIING
I've fallen into one of my own traps!
?!
© Peyo
3

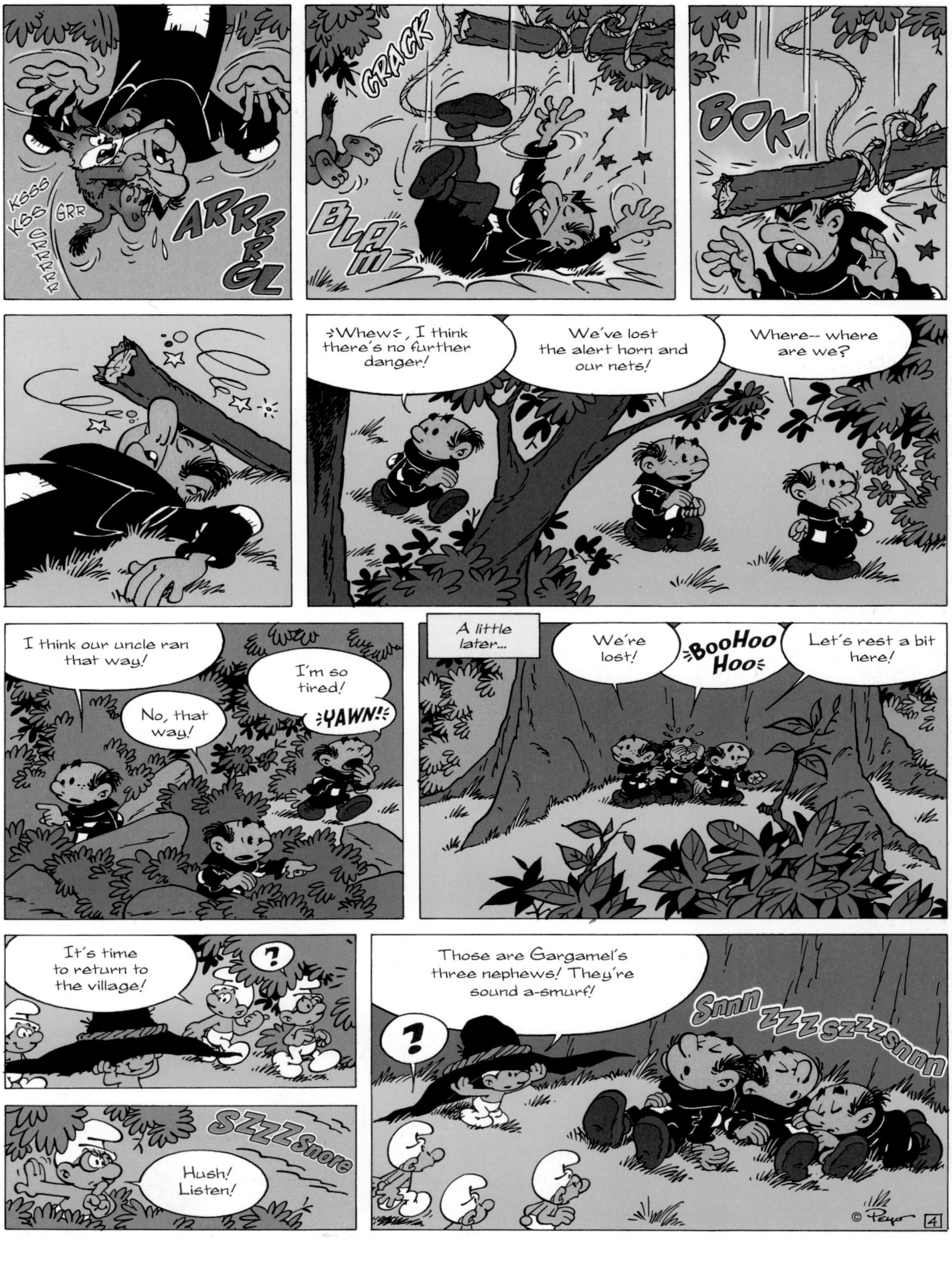
KSSS KSS GRRRRR
GRR
ARRRRRGL
CRACK
BLAM
BOK
Whew, I think there's no further danger!
We've lost the alert horn and our nets!
Where-- where are we?
I think our uncle ran that way!
No, that way!
I'm so tired!
YAWN!
A little later...
We're lost!
BooHoo Hoo
Let's rest a bit here!
It's time to return to the village!
?
Hush! Listen!
SZZZ Snore
Those are Gargamel's three nephews! They're sound a-smurf!
?
Snnn ZZZ SZZZSNNNN
© Peyo
4

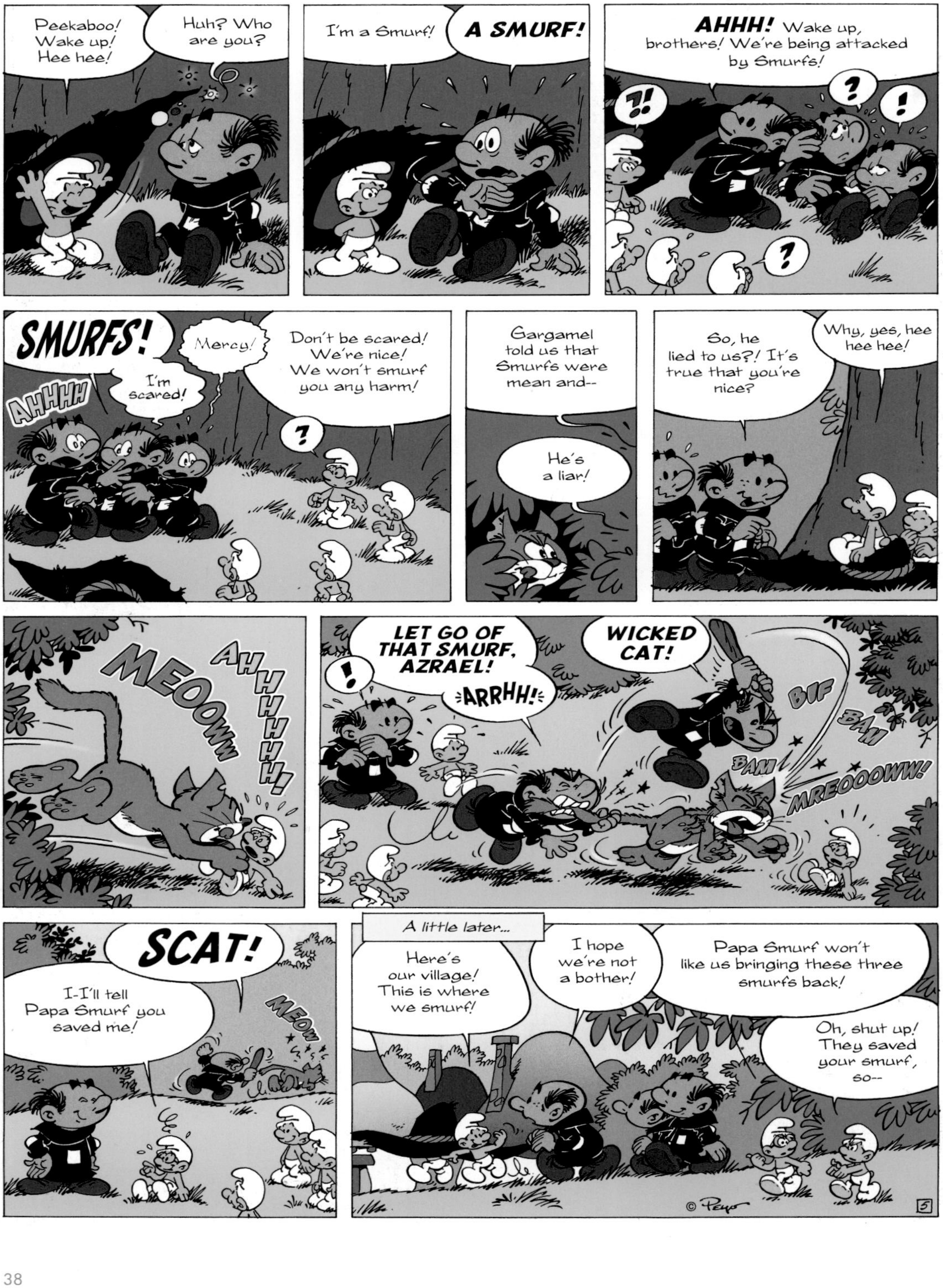

Peekaboo! Wake up! Hee hee!
Huh? Who are you?
I'm a Smurf!
A SMURF!
AHHH! Wake up, brothers! We're being attacked by Smurfs!
?!
?
!
?
SMURFS!
AHHHH
Mercy!
I'm scared!
Don't be scared! We're nice! We won't smurf you any harm!
?
Gargamel told us that Smurfs were mean and--
He's a liar!
So, he lied to us?! It's true that you're nice?
Why, yes, hee hee hee!
MEOOWW
AHHHHHHH!
LET GO OF THAT SMURF, AZRAEL!
!
ARRHH!
WICKED CAT!
BIF
BAM
BAM
MREOOOWW!
SCAT!
I-I'll tell Papa Smurf you saved me!
MEOW
A little later...
Here's our village! This is where we smurf!
I hope we're not a bother!
Papa Smurf won't like us bringing these three smurfs back!
Oh, shut up! They saved your smurf, so--
© Peyo
5

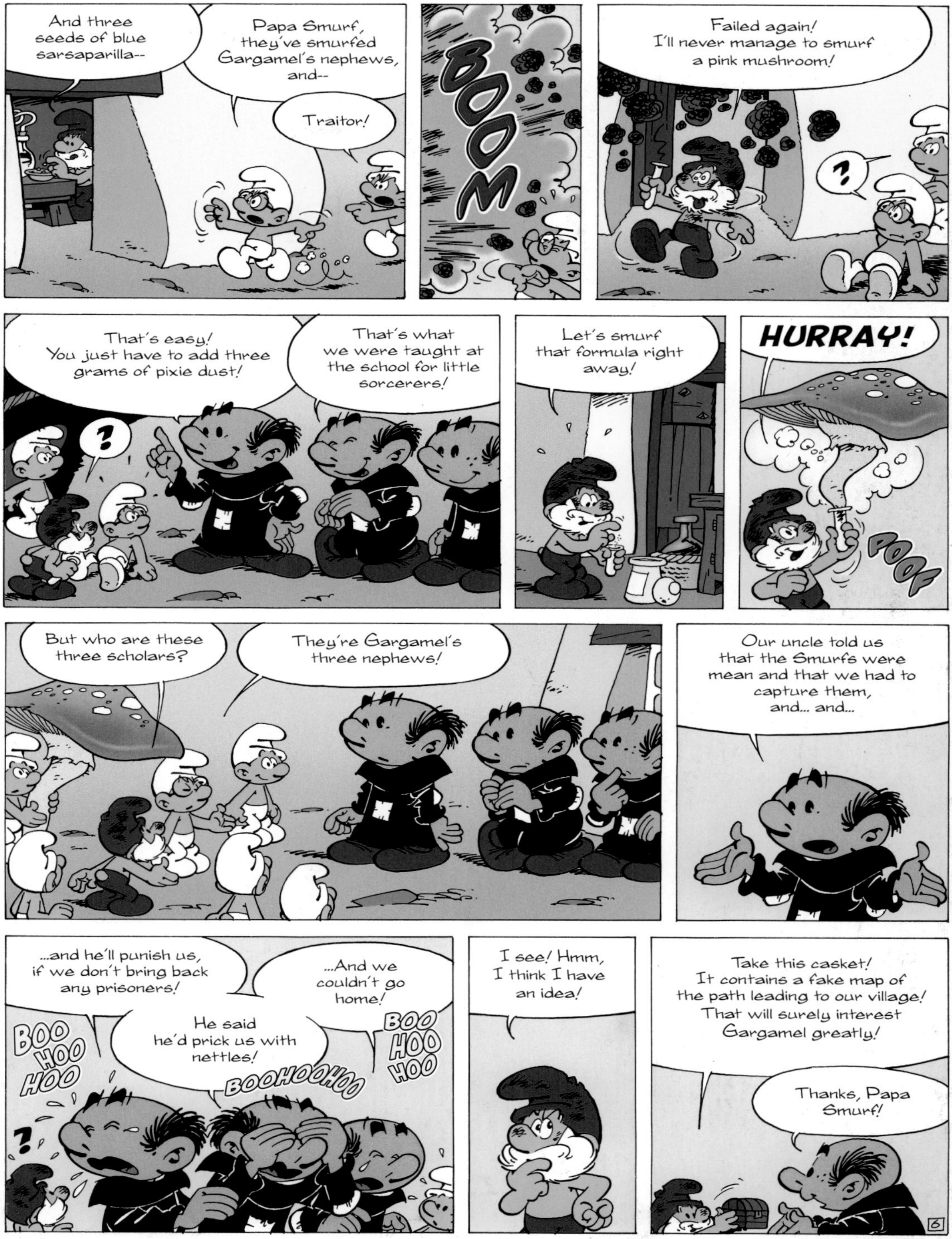
And three seeds of blue sarsaparilla--
Papa Smurf, they've smurfed Gargamel's nephews, and--
Traitor!
BOOM
Failed again! I'll never manage to smurf a pink mushroom!
?
That's easy! You just have to add three grams of pixie dust!
?
That's what we were taught at the school for little sorcerers!
Let's smurf that formula right away!
HURRAY!
POOF
But who are these three scholars?
They're Gargamel's three nephews!
Our uncle told us that the Smurfs were mean and that we had to capture them, and... and...
...and he'll punish us, if we don't bring back any prisoners!
BOO HOO HOO
He said he'd prick us with nettles!
BOOHOOHOO
...And we couldn't go home!
BOO HOO HOO
?
I see! Hmm, I think I have an idea!
Take this casket! It contains a fake map of the path leading to our village! That will surely interest Gargamel greatly!
Thanks, Papa Smurf!
6

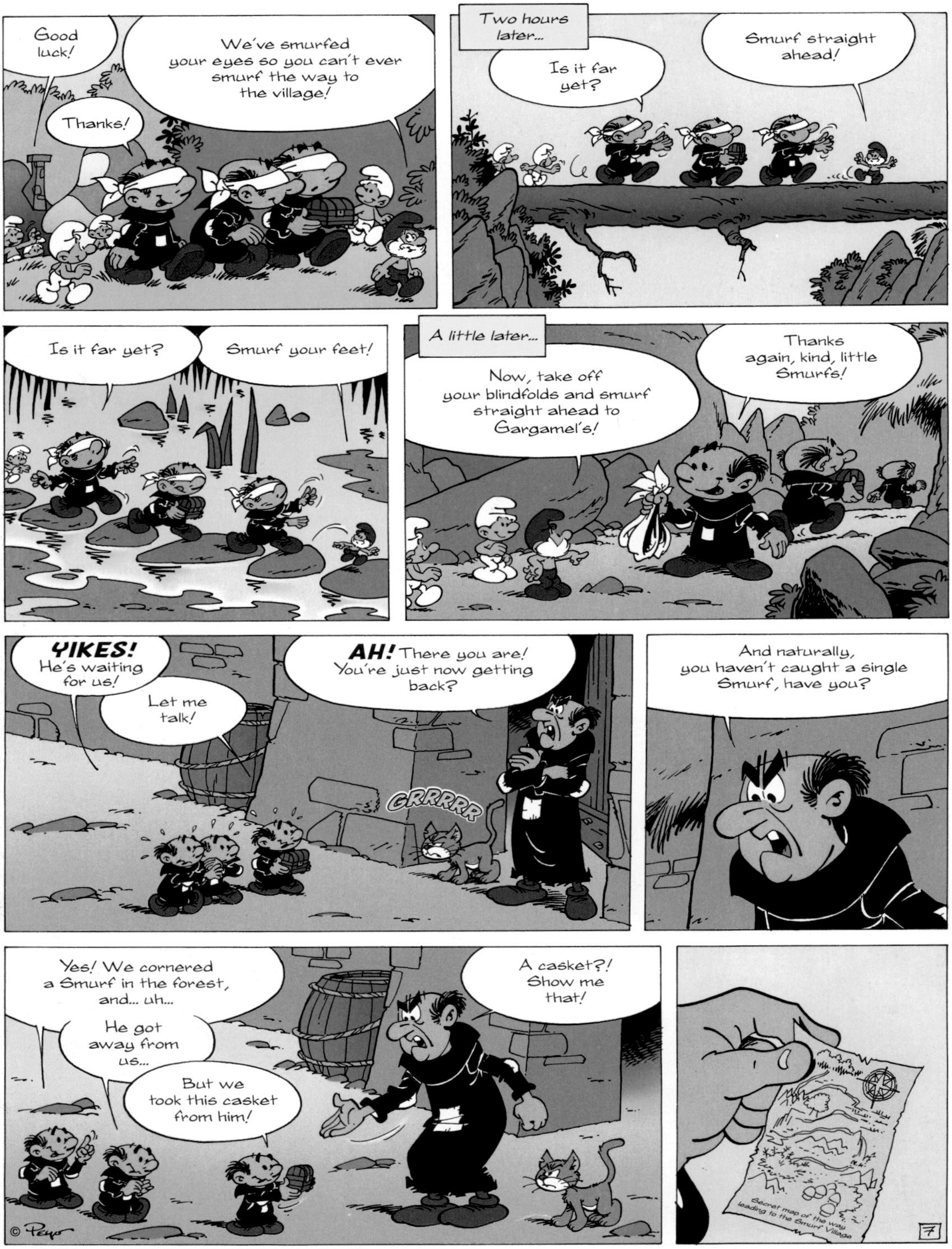
Good luck!
We've smurfed your eyes so you can't ever smurf the way to the village!
Thanks!
Two hours later...
Is it far yet?
Smurf straight ahead!
Is it far yet?
Smurf your feet!
A little later...
Now, take off your blindfolds and smurf straight ahead to Gargamel's!
Thanks again, kind, little Smurfs!
YIKES! He's waiting for us!
Let me talk!
AH! There you are! You're just now getting back?
GRRRRR
And naturally, you haven't caught a single Smurf, have you?
Yes! We cornered a Smurf in the forest, and... uh...
He got away from us...
But we took this casket from him!
A casket?! Show me that!
Secret map of the way leading to the Smurf Village
7
© Peyo

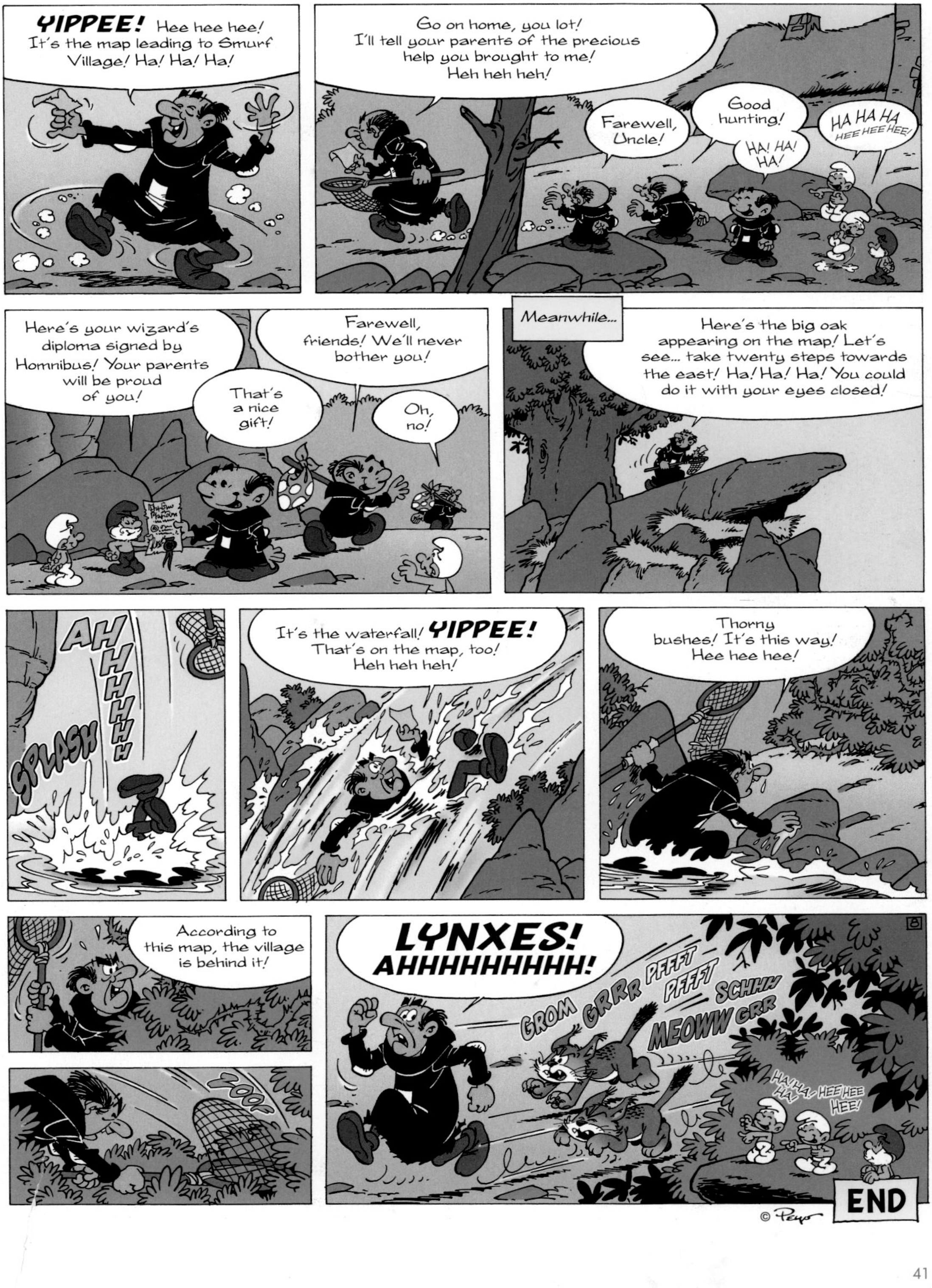
YIPPEE! Hee hee hee! It's the map leading to Smurf Village! Ha! Ha! Ha!
Go on home, you lot! I'll tell your parents of the precious help you brought to me! Heh heh heh!
Farewell, Uncle!
Good hunting!
HA! HA! HA!
HA HA HA HEE HEE HEE!
Here's your wizard's diploma signed by Homnibus! Your parents will be proud of you!
That's a nice gift!
Farewell, friends! We'll never bother you!
Oh, no!
Meanwhile...
Here's the big oak appearing on the map! Let's see... take twenty steps towards the east! Ha! Ha! Ha! You could do it with your eyes closed!
AHHHHHHHH
SPLASH
It's the waterfall! YIPPEE! That's on the map, too! Heh heh heh!
Thorny bushes! It's this way! Hee hee hee!
According to this map, the village is behind it!
ZOOF
8
LYNXES! AHHHHHHHHH!
GROM GRRR PFFFT PFFFT SCHHH MEOWW GRR
HA! HA! HA! HEE! HEE HEE!
END
© Peyo

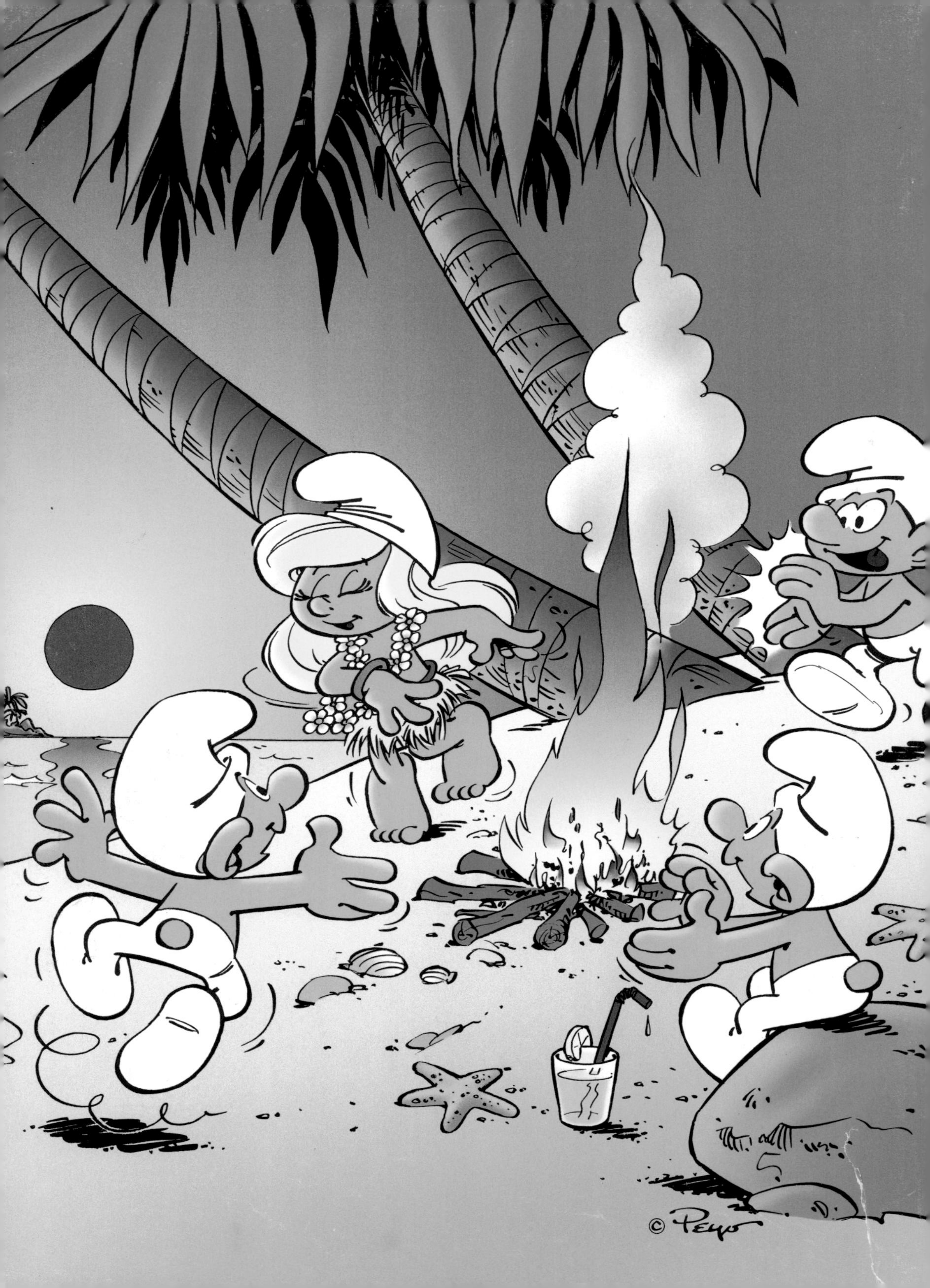
© Peyo

SMURF SURFING

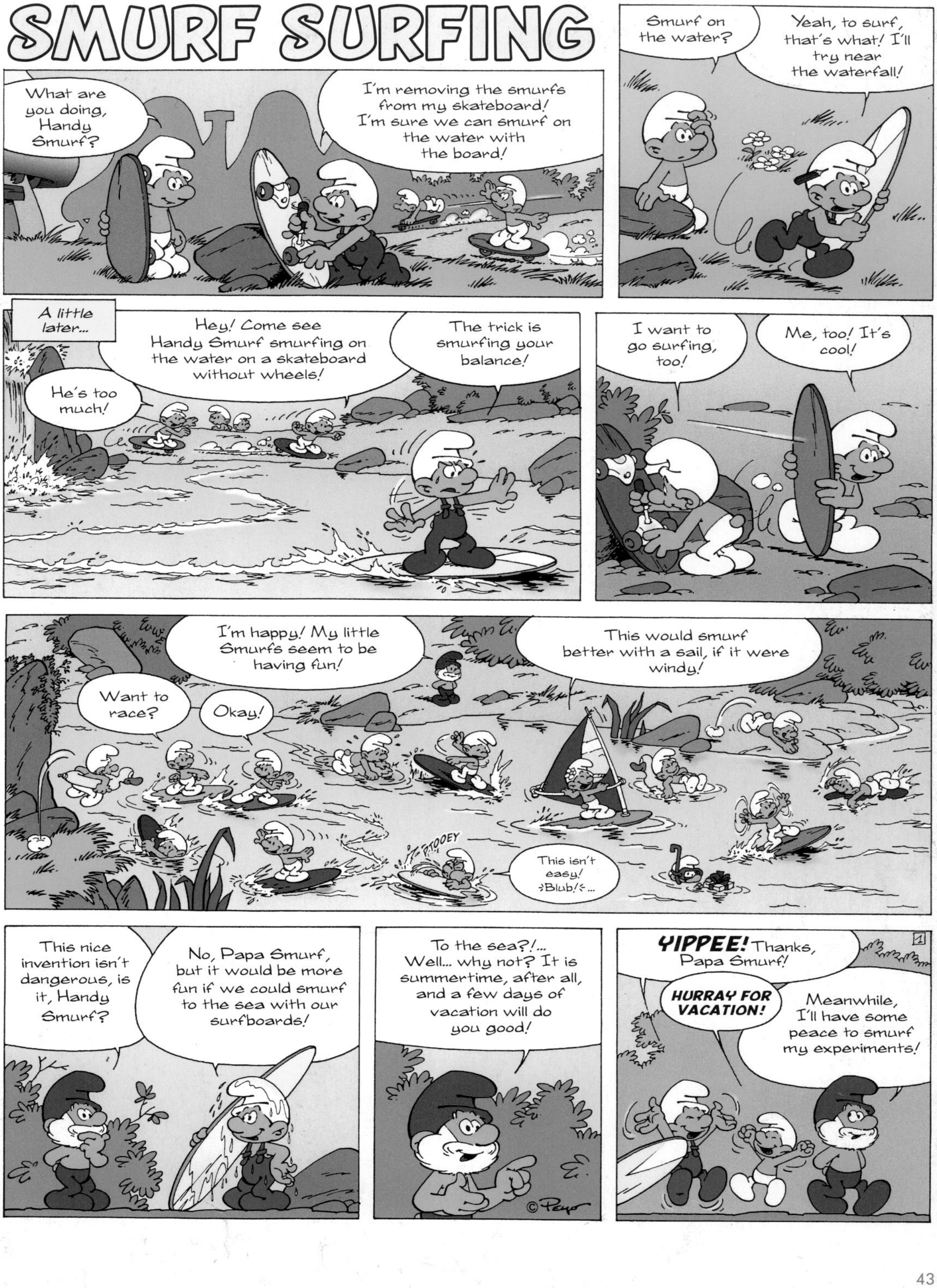

What are you doing, Handy Smurf?
I'm removing the smurfs from my skateboard! I'm sure we can smurf on the water with the board!
Smurf on the water?
Yeah, to surf, that's what! I'll try near the waterfall!
A little later...
He's too much!
Hey! Come see Handy Smurf smurfing on the water on a skateboard without wheels!
The trick is smurfing your balance!
I want to go surfing, too!
Me, too! It's cool!
I'm happy! My little Smurfs seem to be having fun!
This would smurf better with a sail, if it were windy!
Want to race?
Okay!
P-TOOEY
This isn't easy! ›Blub!‹ ...
This nice invention isn't dangerous, is it, Handy Smurf?
No, Papa Smurf, but it would be more fun if we could smurf to the sea with our surfboards!
To the sea?!... Well... why not? It is summertime, after all, and a few days of vacation will do you good!
YIPPEE! Thanks, Papa Smurf!
1
HURRAY FOR VACATION!
Meanwhile, I'll have some peace to smurf my experiments!
© Peyo

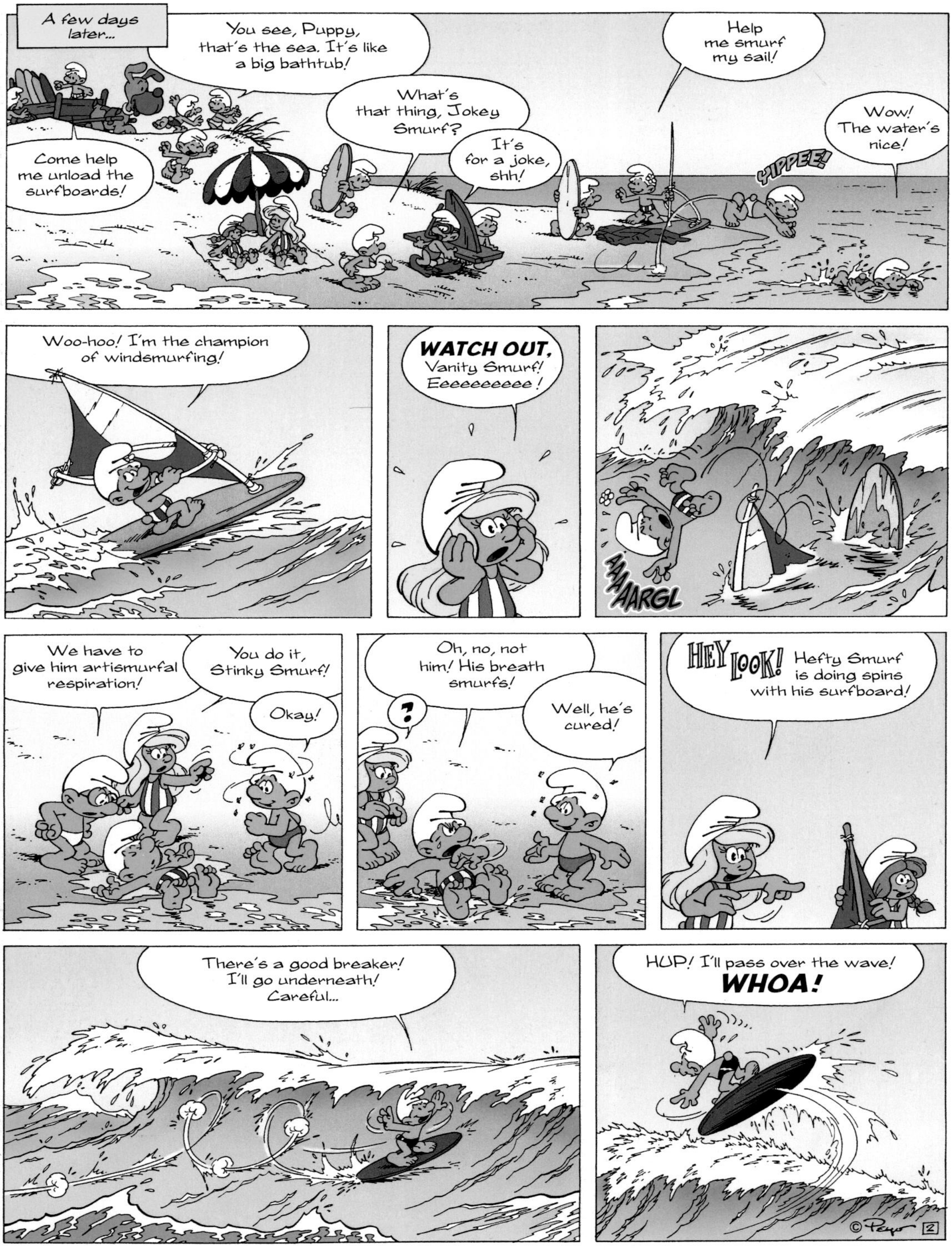
A few days later...
You see, Puppy, that's the sea. It's like a big bathtub!
Come help me unload the surfboards!
What's that thing, Jokey Smurf?
It's for a joke, shh!
Help me smurf my sail!
YIPPEE!
Wow! The water's nice!
Woo-hoo! I'm the champion of windsmurfing!
WATCH OUT, Vanity Smurf! Eeeeeeeeee!
AAAAARGL
We have to give him artismurfal respiration!
You do it, Stinky Smurf!
Okay!
?
Oh, no, not him! His breath smurfs!
Well, he's cured!
HEY LOOK! Hefty Smurf is doing spins with his surfboard!
There's a good breaker! I'll go underneath! Careful...
HUP! I'll pass over the wave! WHOA!
© Peyo
2

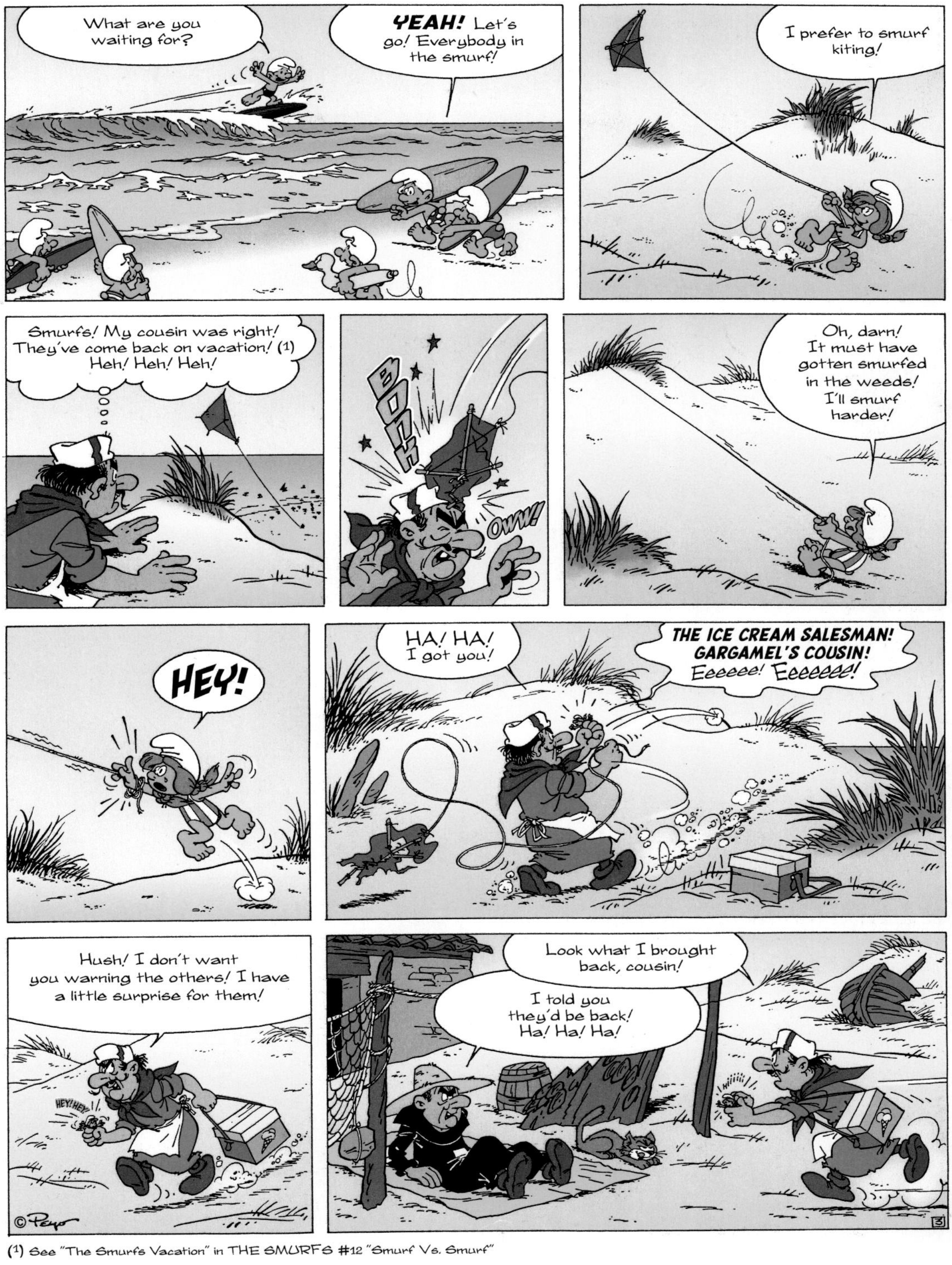
What are you waiting for?
YEAH! Let's go! Everybody in the smurf!
I prefer to smurf kiting!
Smurfs! My cousin was right! They've come back on vacation! (1) Heh! Heh! Heh!
BONK
OWW!
Oh, darn! It must have gotten smurfed in the weeds! I'll smurf harder!
HEY!
HA! HA! I got you!
THE ICE CREAM SALESMAN! GARGAMEL'S COUSIN! Eeeeee! Eeeeeee!
Hush! I don't want you warning the others! I have a little surprise for them!
HEY! HEY!
© Peyo
Look what I brought back, cousin!
I told you they'd be back! Ha! Ha! Ha!
3

(1) See "The Smurfs Vacation" in THE SMURFS #12 "Smurf Vs. Smurf"

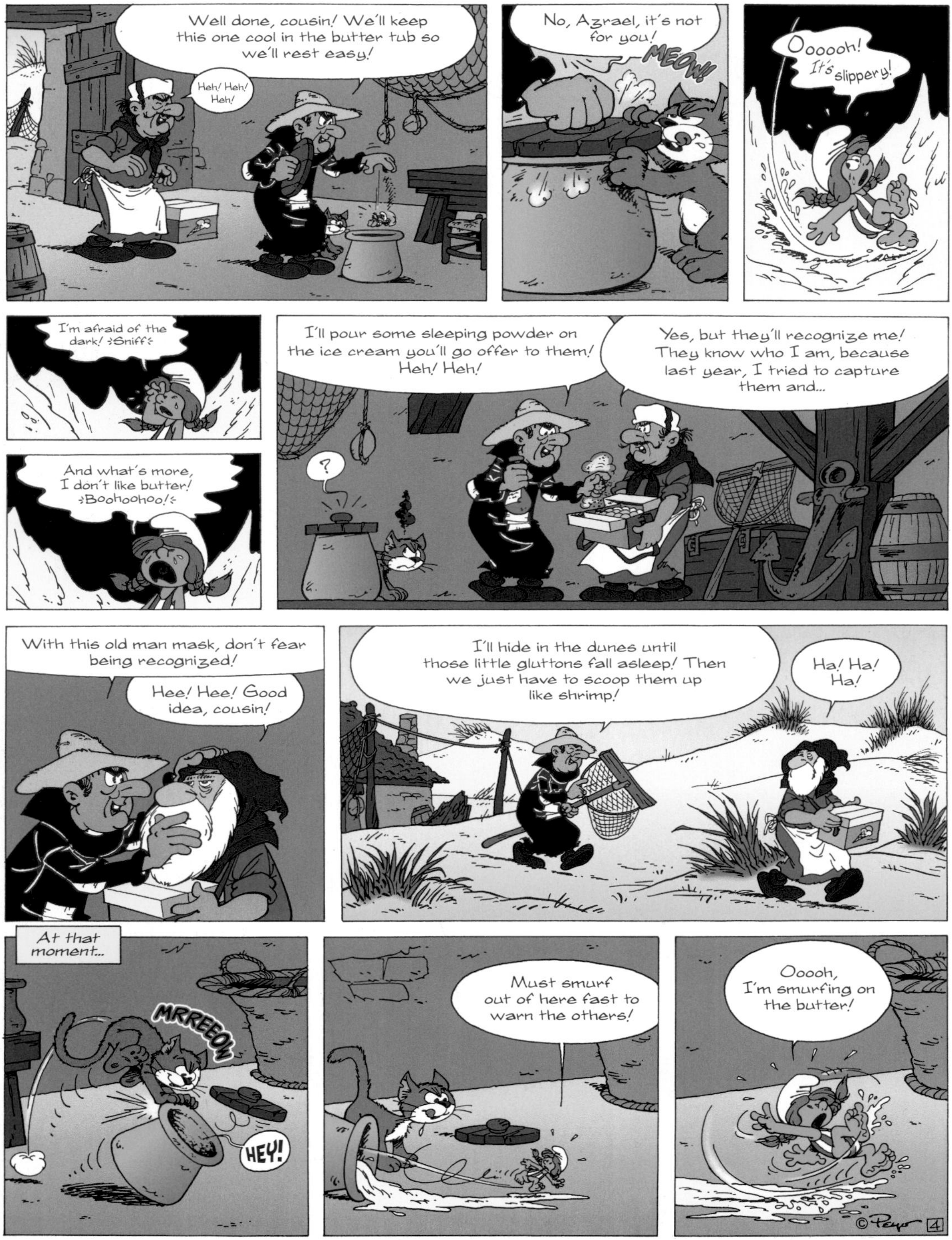
Well done, cousin! We'll keep this one cool in the butter tub so we'll rest easy!
Heh! Heh! Heh!
No, Azrael, it's not for you!
MEOW!
Oooooh! It's slippery!
I'm afraid of the dark! *Sniff*
And what's more, I don't like butter! *Boohoohoo!*
I'll pour some sleeping powder on the ice cream you'll go offer to them! Heh! Heh!
Yes, but they'll recognize me! They know who I am, because last year, I tried to capture them and...
?
With this old man mask, don't fear being recognized!
Hee! Hee! Good idea, cousin!
I'll hide in the dunes until those little gluttons fall asleep! Then we just have to scoop them up like shrimp!
Ha! Ha! Ha!
At that moment...
MRREEEOW
HEY!
Must smurf out of here fast to warn the others!
Ooooh, I'm smurfing on the butter!
© Peyo
4

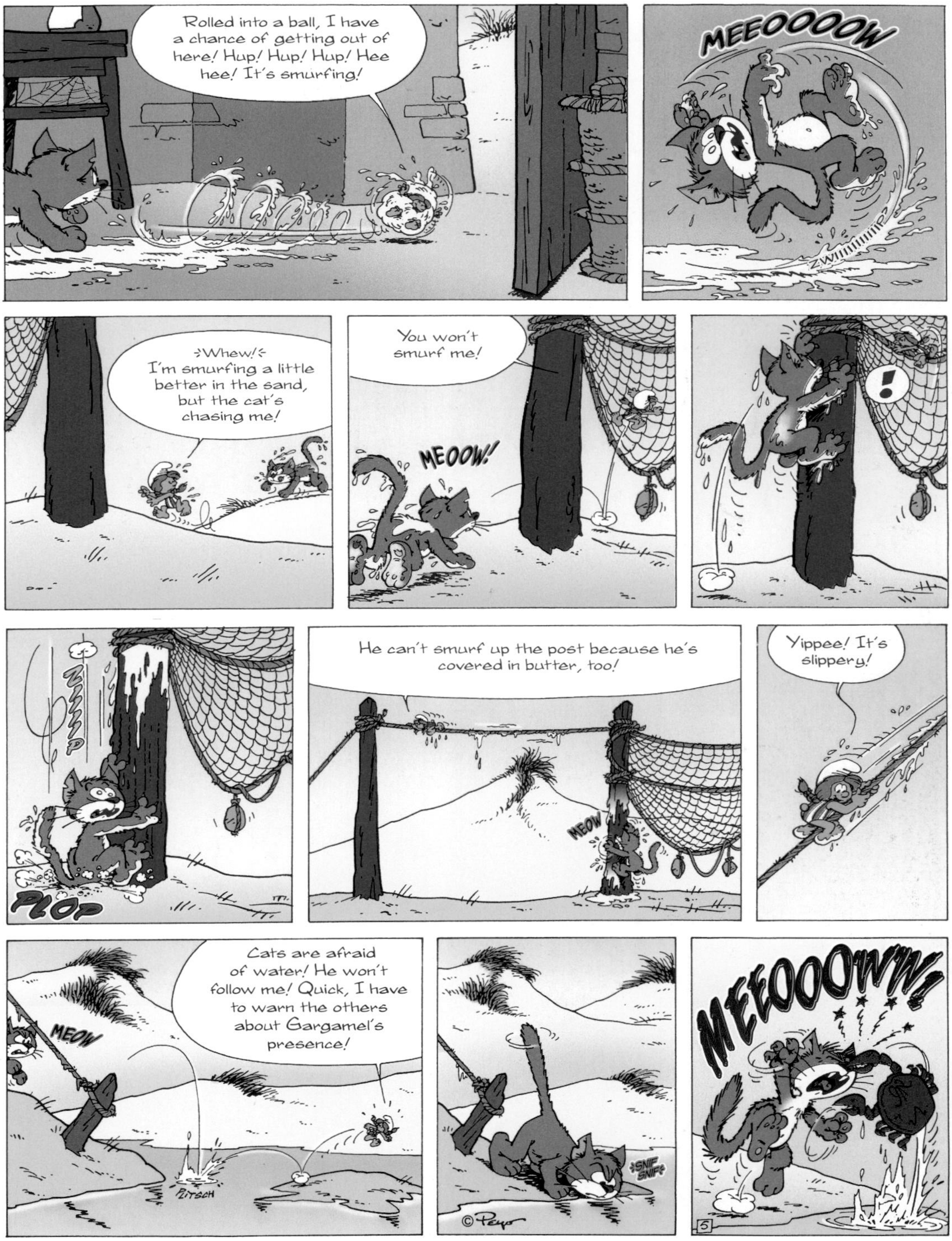
Rolled into a ball, I have a chance of getting out of here! Hup! Hup! Hup! Hee hee! It's smurfing!
MEEOOOOW
Whew! I'm smurfing a little better in the sand, but the cat's chasing me!
You won't smurf me!
MEOOW!
!
PLOP
He can't smurf up the post because he's covered in butter, too!
MEOW
Yippee! It's slippery!
MEOW
Cats are afraid of water! He won't follow me! Quick, I have to warn the others about Gargamel's presence!
PLITSCH
SNIF SNIF
© Peyo
MEEOOOWW!
5

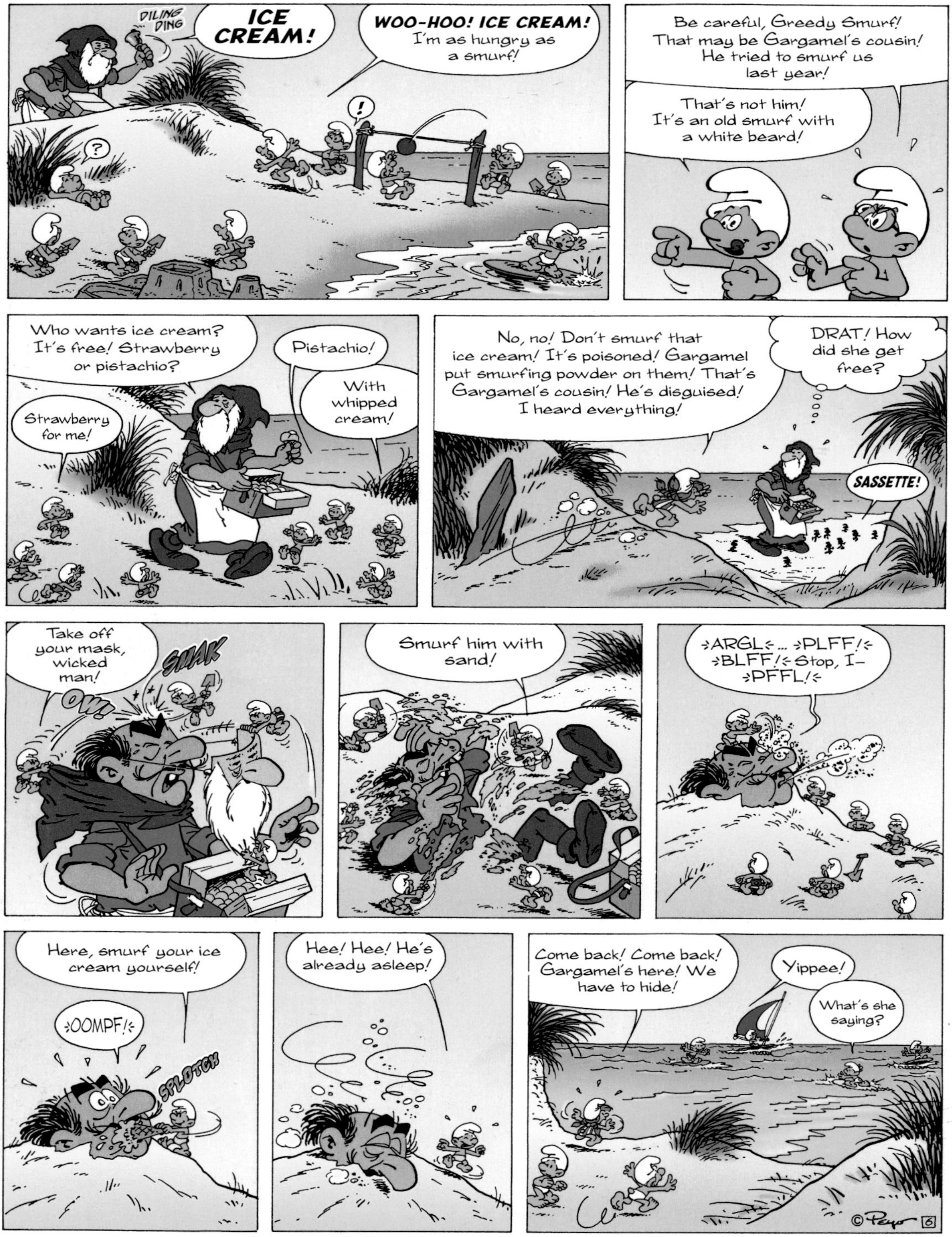

DILING DING
ICE CREAM!
WOO-HOO! ICE CREAM! I'm as hungry as a smurf!
!
?
Be careful, Greedy Smurf! That may be Gargamel's cousin! He tried to smurf us last year!
That's not him! It's an old smurf with a white beard!
Who wants ice cream? It's free! Strawberry or pistachio?
Pistachio!
With whipped cream!
Strawberry for me!
No, no! Don't smurf that ice cream! It's poisoned! Gargamel put smurfing powder on them! That's Gargamel's cousin! He's disguised! I heard everything!
DRAT! How did she get free?
SASSETTE!
Take off your mask, wicked man!
SMAK
OW!
Smurf him with sand!
ARGL... PLFF! BLFF! Stop, I— PFFL!
Here, smurf your ice cream yourself!
OOMPF!
SPLOTCH
Hee! Hee! He's already asleep!
Come back! Come back! Gargamel's here! We have to hide!
Yippee!
What's she saying?
© Peyo
6

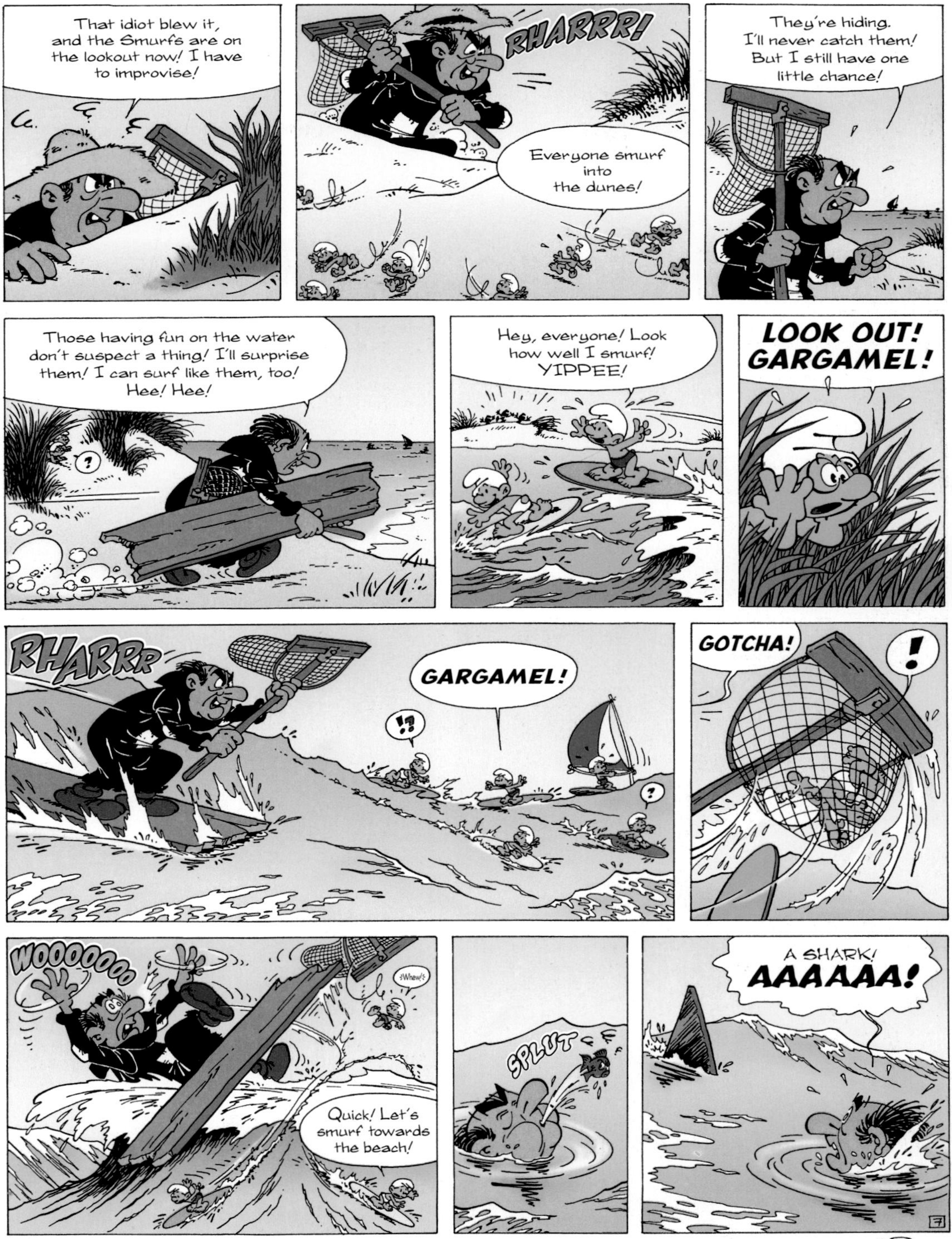
That idiot blew it, and the Smurfs are on the lookout now! I have to improvise!
RHARRR!
Everyone smurf into the dunes!
They're hiding. I'll never catch them! But I still have one little chance!
Those having fun on the water don't suspect a thing! I'll surprise them! I can surf like them, too! Hee! Hee!
?
Hey, everyone! Look how well I smurf! YIPPEE!
LOOK OUT! GARGAMEL!
RHARRR
GARGAMEL!
!?
?
GOTCHA!
!
WOOOOOOO
Whew!
Quick! Let's smurf towards the beach!
SPLUT
A SHARK! AAAAAA!
7
©Peyo

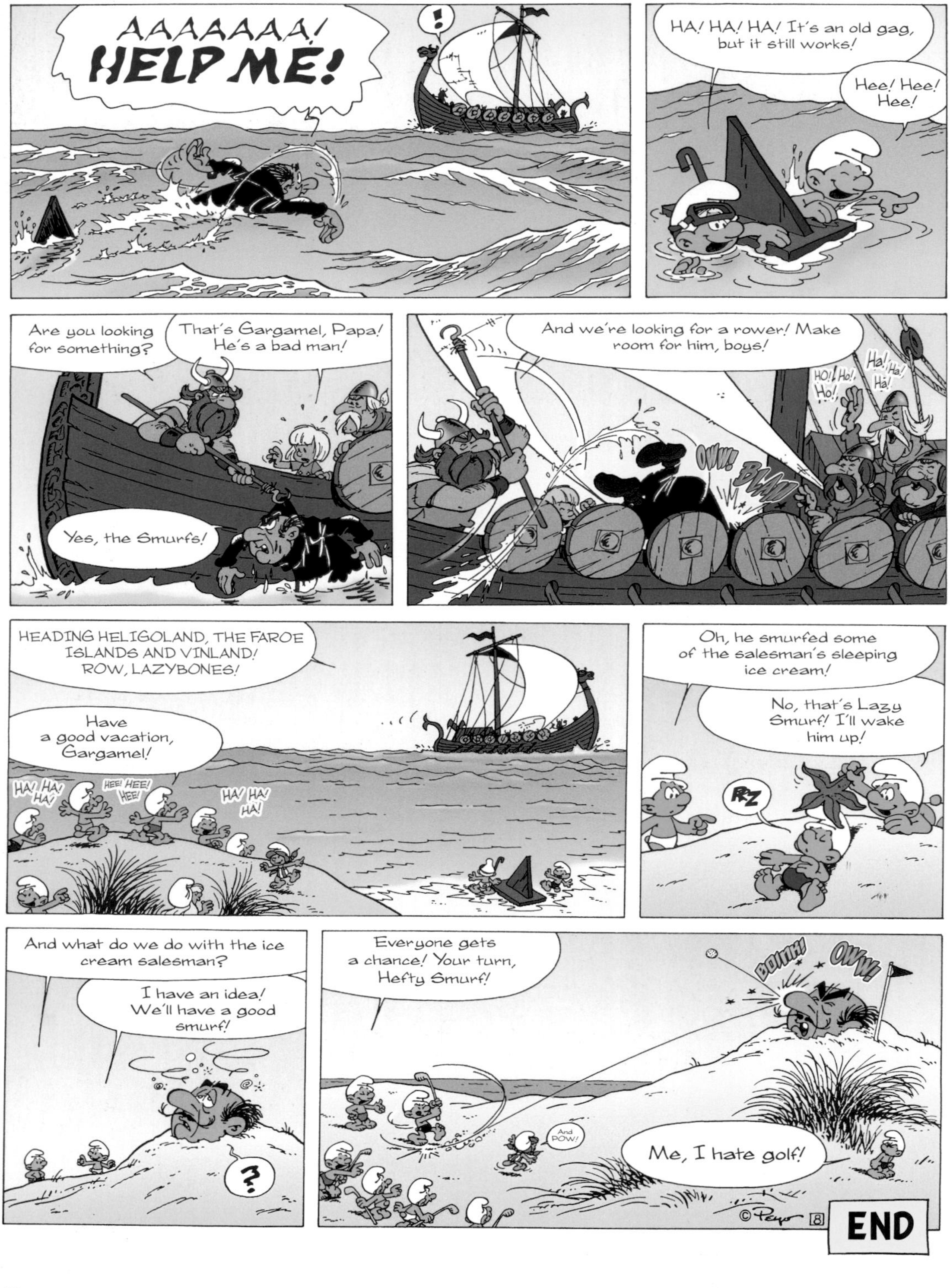
AAAAAAA! HELP ME!
!
HA! HA! HA! It's an old gag, but it still works!
Hee! Hee! Hee!
Are you looking for something?
That's Gargamel, Papa! He's a bad man!
Yes, the Smurfs!
And we're looking for a rower! Make room for him, boys!
HO! Ho! Ho!
Ha! Ha! Ha!
OWW!
BLAM!
HEADING HELIGOLAND, THE FAROE ISLANDS AND VINLAND! ROW, LAZYBONES!
Have a good vacation, Gargamel!
HA! HA! HA!
HEE! HEE! HEE!
HA! HA! HA!
Oh, he smurfed some of the salesman's sleeping ice cream!
No, that's Lazy Smurf! I'll wake him up!
RZ
And what do we do with the ice cream salesman?
I have an idea! We'll have a good smurf!
?
Everyone gets a chance! Your turn, Hefty Smurf!
BOINNG!
OWW!
And POW!
Me, I hate golf!
© Peyo 8
END

WATCH OUT FOR PAPERCUTZ™

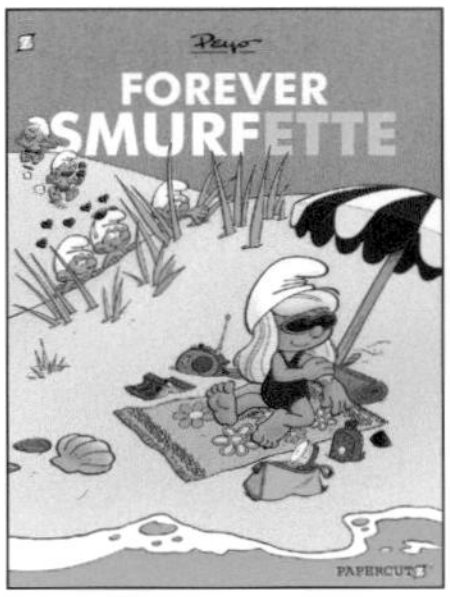
Peyo
FOREVER SMURFETTE
PAPERCUTZ

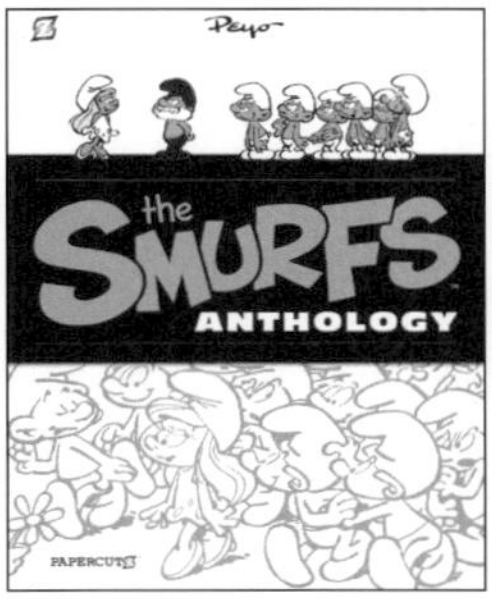
Peyo
the SMURFS
ANTHOLOGY
PAPERCUTZ

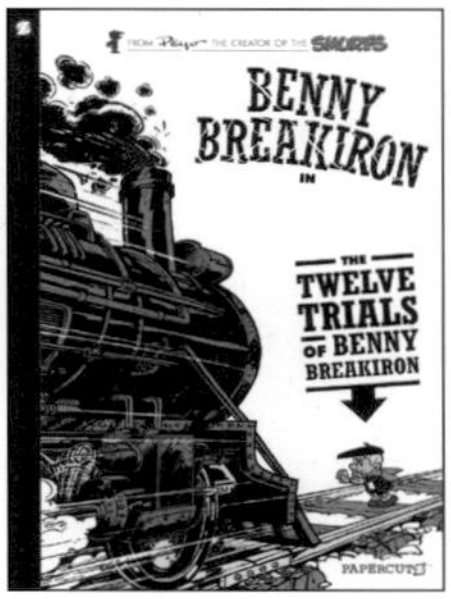
BENNY BREAKIRON
IN
THE TWELVE TRIALS OF BENNY BREAKIRON
PAPERCUTZ

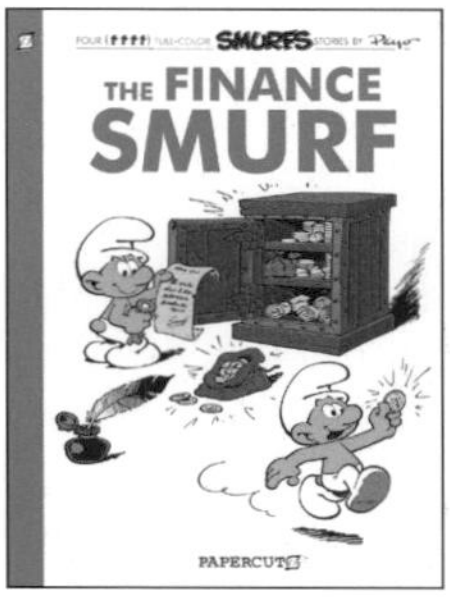
THE FINANCE SMURF
PAPERCUTZ

Welcome to the somewhat family-stuffed seventeenth SMURFS graphic novel by Peyo from Papercutz, the family-like company dedicated to publishing great graphic novels for all ages. I'm Jim Salicrup, the Smurf-in-Chief, here to mention a few Smurf and/or Peyo related items of interest...

Response to THE SMURFS CHRISTMAS graphic novel has been so positive, that we're publishing another SMURFS special—FOREVER SMURFETTE! The Smurfette is always super-popular—THE SMURFS #4 and #10, which star the blue bombshell, are two of our biggest smurfsellers—so it only makes sense to give her a special graphic novel all her own! Look for it wherever Smurfs are sold!

More good news, THE SMURFS ANTHOLOGY is also another success story! For those of you who wonder why you might want to pick up these larger deluxe editions of the early SMURFS stories, the answer is that SMURFS ANTHOLOGY also features the adventures of *Johan and Peewit*. That's the series where the Smurfs first appeared, featuring a brave page and a court jester. The Johan and Peewit stories are just as much fun as THE SMURFS, after all it's also from Peyo! In fact, the Smurfs hardly appear at all in the story featured in THE SMURFS ANTHOLOGY #2, but we think you'll really like it. See for yourself, as we provide a peek at "The War of the 7 Springs," by Yvan Delporte and Peyo on the following pages.

And lest we forget our other Peyo-created graphic novel series, be sure to pick up the latest BENNY BREAKIRON graphic novel—"The Twelve Trials of Benny Breakiron"! This one, also written by Yvan Delporte, is one of the most action-packed graphic novels Papercutz has ever published!

Finally, for those of you who wondered about the Smurf economy, you won't want to miss THE SMURFS #18 "The Finance Smurf." While you and I may have to struggle in these difficult times to make ends meet—the Smurfs seem to have figured out how to not only survive, but to thrive! You won't want to miss it!

Smurf you later,

Jim

STAY IN TOUCH!

EMAIL: Salicrup@papercutz.com
WEB: www.papercutz.com
TWITTER: @papercutzgn
FACEBOOK: PAPERCUTZGRAPHICNOVELS
SNAIL MAIL: Papercutz, 160 Broadway, Suite 700, East Wing, New York, NY 10038

THE WAR OF THE 7 SPRINGS

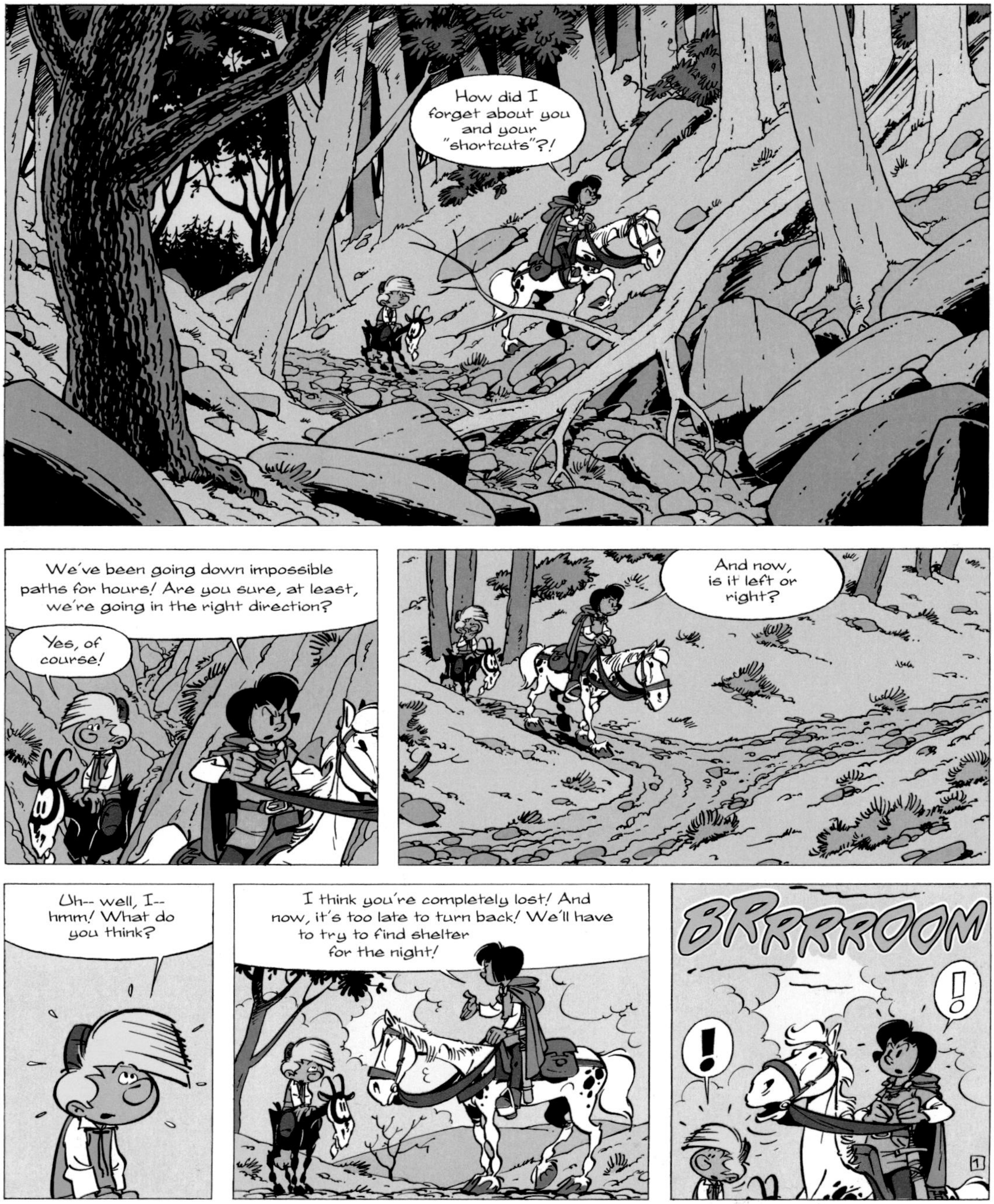
How did I forget about you and your "shortcuts"?!
We've been going down impossible paths for hours! Are you sure, at least, we're going in the right direction?
Yes, of course!
And now, is it left or right?
Uh-- well, I-- hmm! What do you think?
I think you're completely lost! And now, it's too late to turn back! We'll have to try to find shelter for the night!
BRRRROOM
!
!
1

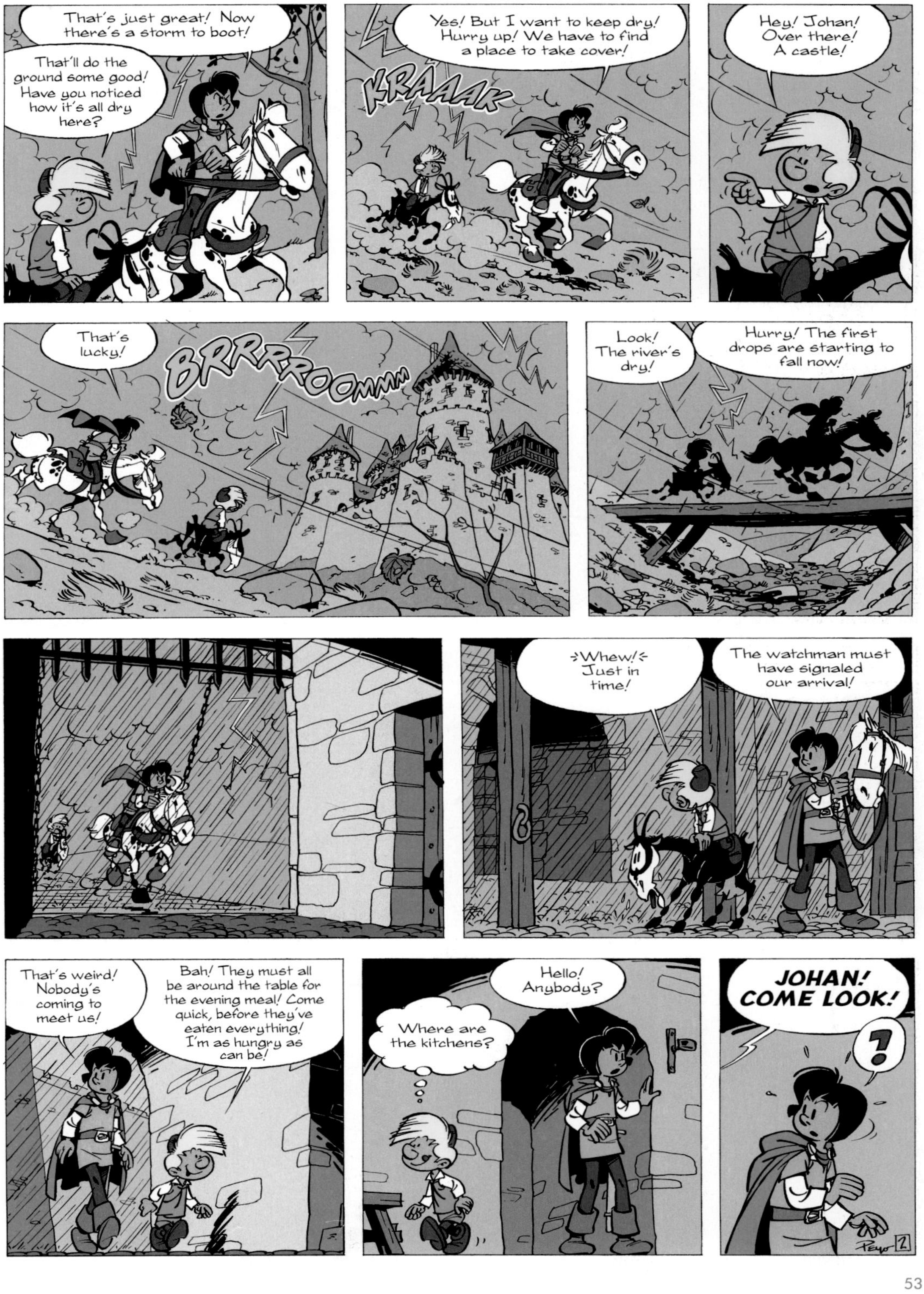

That's just great! Now there's a storm to boot!
That'll do the ground some good! Have you noticed how it's all dry here?
Yes! But I want to keep dry! Hurry up! We have to find a place to take cover!
KRAAAK
Hey! Johan! Over there! A castle!
That's lucky!
BRRRROOMMM
Look! The river's dry!
Hurry! The first drops are starting to fall now!
Whew! Just in time!
The watchman must have signaled our arrival!
That's weird! Nobody's coming to meet us!
Bah! They must all be around the table for the evening meal! Come quick, before they've eaten everything! I'm as hungry as can be!
Hello! Anybody?
Where are the kitchens?
JOHAN! COME LOOK!
?
Peyo 2

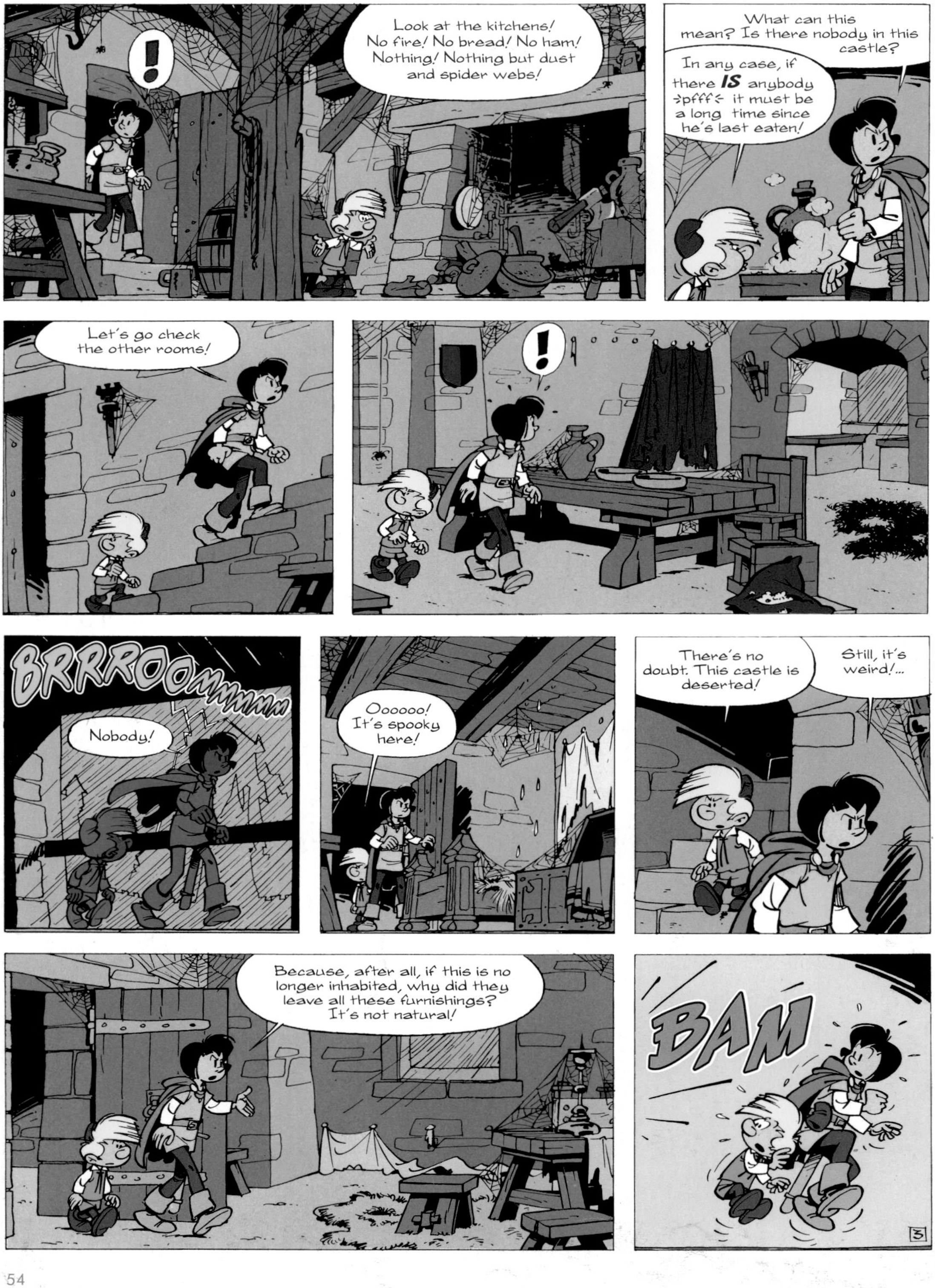
!
Look at the kitchens! No fire! No bread! No ham! Nothing! Nothing but dust and spider webs!
What can this mean? Is there nobody in this castle?
In any case, if there IS anybody >pfff< it must be a long time since he's last eaten!
Let's go check the other rooms!
!
BRRROOMMMMM
Nobody!
Oooooo! It's spooky here!
There's no doubt. This castle is deserted!
Still, it's weird!...
Because, after all, if this is no longer inhabited, why did they leave all these furnishings? It's not natural!
BAM
3

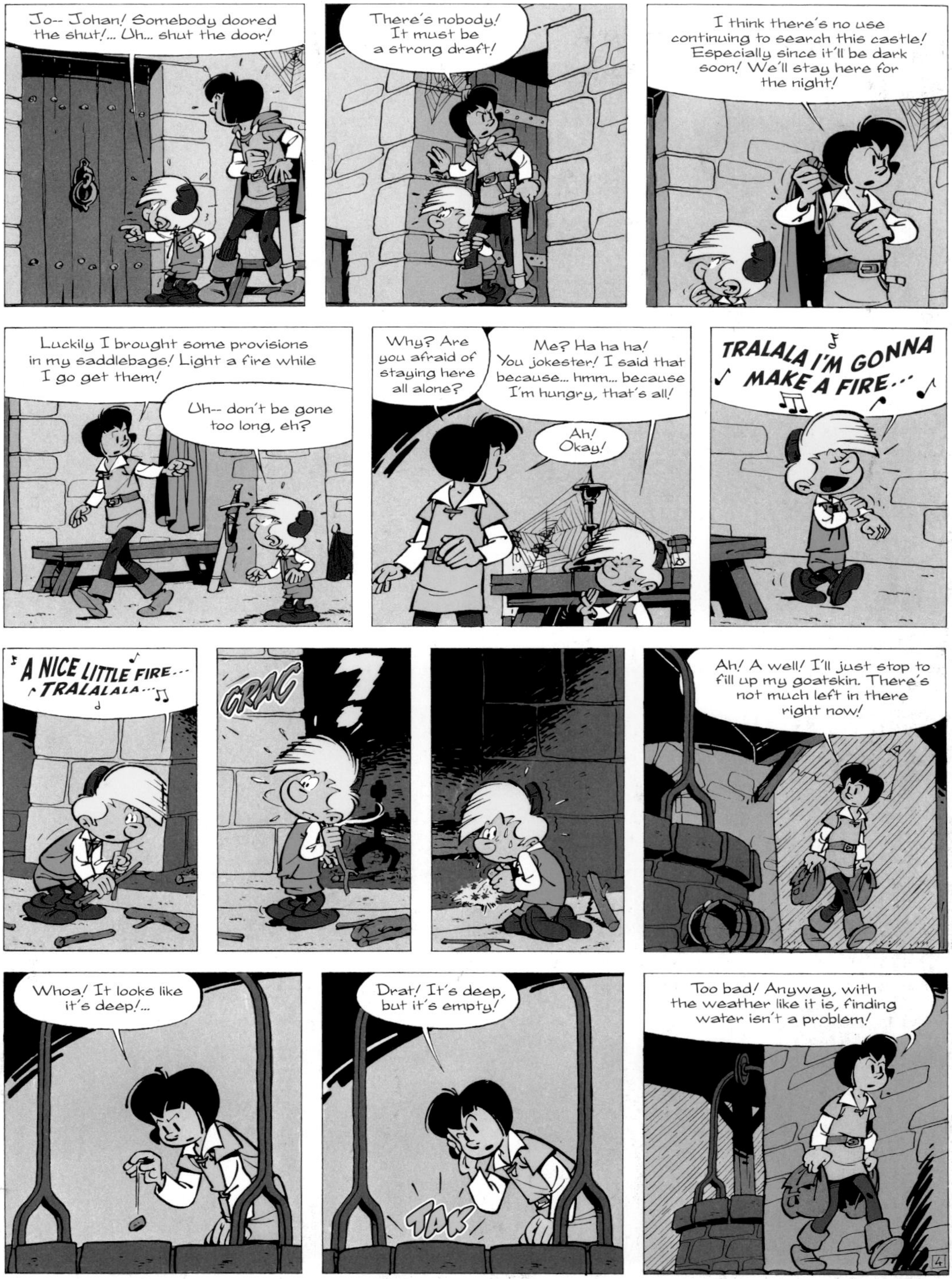
Jo-- Johan! Somebody doored the shut!... Uh... shut the door!
There's nobody! It must be a strong draft!
I think there's no use continuing to search this castle! Especially since it'll be dark soon! We'll stay here for the night!
Luckily I brought some provisions in my saddlebags! Light a fire while I go get them!
Uh-- don't be gone too long, eh?
Why? Are you afraid of staying here all alone?
Me? Ha ha ha! You jokester! I said that because... hmm... because I'm hungry, that's all!
Ah! Okay!
TRALALA I'M GONNA MAKE A FIRE...
A NICE LITTLE FIRE... TRALALALA...
CRAC
Ah! A well! I'll just stop to fill up my goatskin. There's not much left in there right now!
Whoa! It looks like it's deep!...
Drat! It's deep, but it's empty!
TAK
Too bad! Anyway, with the weather like it is, finding water isn't a problem!
4

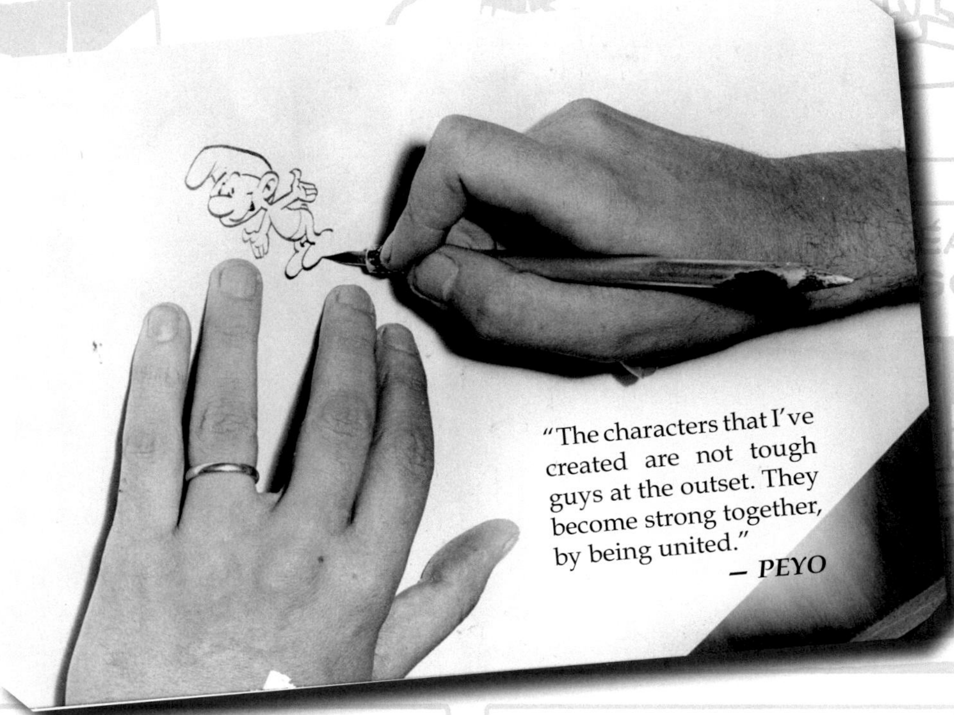

"The characters that I've created are not tough guys at the outset. They become strong together, by being united."

— PEYO

Over 50 years ago, a Belgian cartoonist known as Peyo set his pencil to a blank page and created a worldwide phenomenon we know as The Smurfs. Join us in celebrating more than a half century of humor, camaraderie, heroism, and heart. Experience the master at his best.

THE WONDER OF PEYO

INCOMPARABLE NEW GRAPHIC NOVELS FROM PAPERCUT Z™

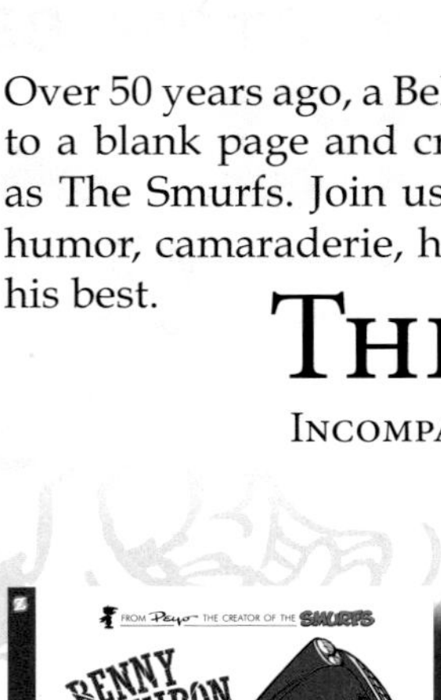

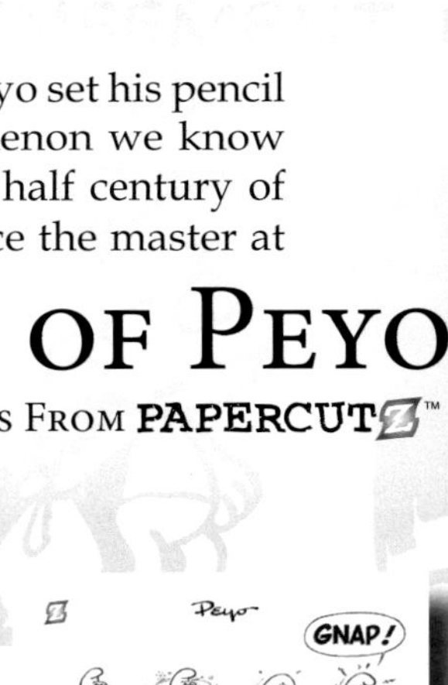